"Is this *rubbish* really essential?"

Without waiting for her response, Matt headed toward the door with her elegant gray vanity case. "That's my property! I want to know what you're going to do!" she shouted as the door swung shut behind him.

For a second she sat stunned, then ran from the house and halted in the yard, staring in horrified disbelief. Matt was throwing her precious cosmetics into the heart of a blazing bonfire.

"Matt—no!" she screamed, leaping at the fire.

"Clea, don't be a fool." Matt's voice was harsh. "Don't you realize that you don't need any of this?"

Driven back by the heat, Clea could only stand and watch numbly. She felt as if a part of her, quite literally, had gone up in smoke.

Kate Walker chose the Brontë sisters, the development of their writing from childhood to maturity, as the topic for her master's thesis. It is little wonder, then, that she should go on to write romance fiction. She lives in the United Kingdom with her husband and son, and when she isn't writing, she tries to keep up with her hobbies of embroidery, knitting, antiques and, of course, reading.

Books by Kate Walker

HARLEQUIN ROMANCE
2783—GAME OF HAZARD
2826—ROUGH DIAMOND
2910—CAPTIVE LOVER
2920—MAN OF SHADOWS

HARLEQUIN PRESENTS
1053—BROKEN SILENCE

The Cinderella Trap

Kate Walker

Harlequin Books

TORONTO • NEW YORK • LONDON
AMSTERDAM • PARIS • SYDNEY • HAMBURG
STOCKHOLM • ATHENS • TOKYO • MILAN

Original hardcover edition published in 1988
by Mills & Boon Limited

ISBN 0-373-02957-8

Harlequin Romance first edition January 1989

For Barbara Malcolm

CHAPTER ONE

'WHICH one's the big man?'

Penny's stage whisper reached Clea clearly even though she was standing several feet away, and she couldn't help smiling at the younger girl's unthinking excitement. If she wasn't careful the 'big man' himself would hear her.

Her smile faded, becoming slightly wry, as she glanced towards the door, seeing the group of people who had just come in and were now being greeted by a small, stout man in a dinner-jacket—the hotel manager probably, Clea decided, the faint twist of her lips becoming more pronounced as she surveyed the fawning deference being shown to the newcomers—and to one man in particular.

Wasn't it obvious which one was Matthew Highland? There was only one man who had owner and managing director of the Highland chain of hotels stamped all over him from the top of his gleaming dark head to the toes of his highly polished hand-made shoes. The only thing that surprised her about him was that he was alone. She would have expected to see some extremely decorative female companion draped on his arm.

'Do you know, Clea?' Penny was at her side, her small, pixieish face alight with excitement.

Clea took a careful sip of her wine and was shocked to find that her hand wasn't quite steady. She had anticipated this moment for weeks, had been preparing for it ever since she had first been told about the ceremonial opening of the Argyle, the newest and most modern Highland hotel, so why should it affect her now that it was actually happening?

'Do you?' Penny prompted impatiently.

'The one on the middle.' Clea gestured slightly with her wine glass.

'The tall dark one?' Penny's eyes were wide blue pools of amazement. 'He's much younger than I thought he would be—and absolutely gorgeous! I never expected he'd look like that!'

No, Clea reflected, she had never anticipated that Matt Highland would be quite so stunningly good-looking either, in fact she had been totally devastated by her first sight of him in that photograph, and again when Barry had brought him home for a visit and she had seen him in the flesh. But that had been so many years ago, when she had been younger than Penny was now, little more than a child really. She'd come a long way since then.

Or had she? Clea's bright green eyes clouded slightly as she took another slow sip of her wine, thankful to see that the faint tremor that had so disconcerted her before had disappeared. It had worried her, making her wonder if that other, much younger Clea was not as deeply buried as she had thought but lingered just below the surface, ready to emerge when she least expected it.

'What time is it?' Penny's persistent questioning was becoming vaguely irritating, especially as Clea had a pretty good idea just why she had asked that particular one. She glanced at the slim gold watch on her slender wrist.

'Eight forty-five.'

They were due to be introduced to Matthew Highland at nine o'clock—and it would be nine exactly, if the meticulous precision with which the rest of this function had been organised was anything to go by. From the moment Clea, Penny and the other two girls had arrived at the Argyle they had been organised and directed until she felt like a cog in a machine, incapable of individual thought, a small part in a very large whole—and all this before Matthew Highland, for whom all this had been arranged, had appeared on the scene.

Still, the motto of Highland Hotels was 'Comfort and Efficiency', she mused—and, tonight at least, they were certainly living up to that. She hadn't seen any of the hotel's bedrooms, but if this luxurious dining-room with its ornate chandeliers, thick, soft carpet and matching burgundy velvet curtains was anything to go by they would be bound to enhance the already glowing reputation of this particular chain. And she had to admit that Highland's managing director was a fine example of his own code. His arrival had been planned for eight-thirty, and at eight twenty-nine precisely she had become aware of the subdued bustle and excitement that announced his presence in the main foyer.

'Only a quarter of an hour to go!' Delighted anticipation lifted Penny's voice.

Vaguely Clea murmured something that might have been agreement as she glanced round, looking for somewhere to place her glass. She hadn't finished her wine, but that hardly mattered; a seemingly endless stream of waiters in black trousers, pristine white shirts, bow ties and waistcoats the exact colour of the curtains were circulating with trays laden with full glasses. She could easily get a fresh drink later; right now she needed a few moments' peace and quiet.

Moving smoothly and gracefully in the way that now came naturally to her after long hours of practice in deportment lessons, Clea made her way across the crowded room, oblivious to the number of interested glances turned in her direction. She was used to public interest now; the stares of large numbers of interested spectators no longer troubled her and she had cultivated the ability to shut herself off from the appreciative looks her appearance drew. Several inches taller than the average woman and slim as a racing greyhound, with a sleek cap of shoulder-length jet-black hair, she couldn't easily become just one of a crowd, a fact which had its advantages in her job as a model but could be distinctly awkward when she preferred to remain strictly anonymous.

The ladies' powder-room was as elegant as the hotel's dining-room had led her to expect it would be. Decorated in pale pink and white, it boasted scented soaps, thickly woven towels and even a huge arrangement of fresh flowers whose scent permeated the room. Very nice, Clea commented silently to herself as she crossed to the illuminated vanity unit, her feet in their delicate, high-heeled gold sandals making no sound on the deep-pile carpet. But from the moment she saw her face in the huge, brightly lit mirror every other thought vanished from her mind as she concentrated on the matter in hand, considering her appearance with a critical appraisal that had now become second nature to her.

Her make-up had lasted well in spite of the heat in the overcrowded room, but it could do with a little freshening up, and her lipstick needed renewing. Pulling out the tiny make-up kit she carried with her everywhere, Clea set about the necessary repairs, her hands moving with practised skill as she added colour here, powder there until at last, after another swift glance in the mirror, she decided she was satisfied and turned her attention to her hair.

The thick black bob had been cut by an artist, every shining hair trimmed so that it fell back into place immediately, no matter how she turned her head. Its style had become her trademark, emphasising her almond-shaped, slightly slanting green eyes and making her look like the portraits of the Egyptian queen Cleopatra, a likeness which her agent had been keen to play up when she had first started out in the modelling world.

As she pulled a brush through her hair an uncomfortable sensation like the fluttering of butterfly wings started up in her stomach, making her pause and frown slightly. She wasn't *nervous!* Years of public appearances on the catwalk or at social functions like this had cured her of any form of stage fright, and she certainly wasn't afraid of Matt Highland—not any more. Besides, she doubted that he would remember her—in fact she very much hoped he wouldn't, because the effect she was planning would be ruined if he ever connected Clea Mallory with the seventeen-year-old Patti Donovan he had once known.

Another few seconds to dab fresh perfume, Saint Laurent's 'Y', her long-time favourite, on her pulse points and in the valley between the curves of her breasts revealed by her low-cut gown were all that was needed before she was completely ready, and she stood back and surveyed her reflection with some satisfaction.

Her dress was simplicity itself, a sleeveless, clinging black sheath with a scooped neckline, and over it she wore a loose chiffon jacket on which abstract leafy shapes were picked out in gold and bronze sequins. Their colours were echoed in subtle tones on her eyelids, a soft blusher emphasised her high cheekbones and a matching lipstick coloured her rather wide mouth. She looked exactly what she was, a successful professional model, every inch sleek and well groomed. Clea allowed herself a slight smile which grew into a grin which would have amazed her agent and any of the photographers she worked with, who were more accustomed to her cool, slightly aloof expression.

'Let's see what Matthew Highland makes of me now!' she said aloud with a conspiratorial wink at her reflection.

Althea pounced as soon as Clea re-entered the dining-room. 'Where have you been? I've been looking everywhere for you!'

'I just went to freshen up my make-up.'

'Freshen up—Clea, you *know* you look perfect, you always do! But come on——' She hurried Clea through the crowds to where Penny and the other model, Claire, were waiting. 'Mr Bowen will be bringing Matthew Highland over at any minute.'

'Don't fuss,' soothed Clea. 'It's only just nine.'

Comfort and efficiency—the words echoed in her head as the large grandfather clock in the corner of the room chimed the hour and she saw Matthew Highland's party heading towards them, the man himself easily discernible, his dark head inches above those of his entourage. To her rather disturbed surprise she found that her palms were damp with perspiration, and she smoothed them against the soft material of her dress as she positioned herself beside Althea, last in the line of four.

'And these are the young ladies who will be modelling at tomorrow's fashion show.'

Clea knew that voice, it belonged to Stan Bowen, the man through whom all the arrangements had been made and who had greeted them on their arrival here tonight. The *deputy* manager, she reflected rather cynically. Not for them the attentions of the manager himself—he was too busy with such illustrious beings as the local MP—and of course Matthew Highland himself.

'This is Miss Althea Austin.'

He was very close now, only a few feet away from Clea as he took Althea's hand and murmured a few polite pleasantries. Under cover of her long, thick lashes, Clea's eyes slid to Matt Highland's face. Had he changed very much over the years?

No, time hardly seemed to have affected him at all. Perhaps there were a few faint tracings of lines around his nose and mouth, but essentially the lean planes of his hardboned face were still the same. It was a powerfully masculine face, the strong features, square jaw and firm mouth proclaiming a confidence close to arrogance, a sense of command and a touch of aggression, qualities that had put him where he was at the relatively young age of thirty-four.

He'd filled out a bit too, the lean, almost rangy form Clea remembered having broadened across the chest and shoulders under the beautifully tailored dinner-jacket and immaculate white shirt, but his waist and hips were slim and athletic, showing that he kept himself very fit. The only soft note about him was the silky mane of dark brown hair, a lock of which had fallen forward on to his high forehead, giving him a surprisingly boyish look. But Clea knew better than to let that deceive her.

'And of course the star of the show, Miss Clea Mallory.'

With a jolt Clea realised that the conversation with Althea had ended, the small group of people had moved, and Matthew Highland stood directly in front of her, his hand held out in greeting.

'It's a pleasure to meet you, Miss Mallory.'

Her hand was taken in a firm, strong grip and she struggled with an irreverent desire to curtsy. With his entourage surrounding him, notably the fawning, almost grovelling manager, Matt Highland appeared as little less than royalty.

'Of course your name—and your face—are well known to me already. I'm delighted that you could find the time to fit this particular assignment into your busy schedule.'

'I am pretty well booked up.' Clea's smile was gracious, professionally charming, and directed straight into eyes of so dark a grey that they were almost black. That way he had of looking you straight in the eye when he spoke had disconcerted her when she was seventeen, but not now. Oh no, Mr Highland, nothing you do scares me any more. 'But I couldn't turn down the chance to model Raphael's designs.'

She was pleased with that, it implied that it was the clothes, created by one of the newest and most exciting designers around, that had attracted her to this assignment, not the lure of working for Highland Hotels, however prestigious they might be.

Matt Highland nodded. 'I've seen his work—it's quite stunning.'

Had he recognised her? That direct, keen gaze had been so searching that just for a second Clea felt a shiver of apprehension run down her spine. But no, those dark eyes showed no flicker of recognition and Matt's tone was smoothly urbane, his words just polite social conversation. Clea let her breath escape in a silent sigh of relief and made herself meet those grey eyes with a look that was every bit as direct as Matt's own.

'Yes, his clothes are quite beautiful—and they're a dream to wear.'

'And I'm sure they can only be enhanced by your beauty when you model them.'

Very nice, Mr Highland. Clea lowered her eyelids and inclined her head slightly in a gracious acknowledgement of the skilful compliment. Oh yes, he had all the social graces, his low, slightly husky voice holding a convincing note of sincerity.

'It isn't hard to look good in Raphael's designs,' she returned. 'They'd flatter any woman. He really understands how to enhance the female form.'

'But you need no such flattery.' Matt's tone had altered subtly and his eyes were bold as they swept over her, moving down from her face and lingering over other, more intimate areas of her body. It wasn't hard to read his mind. Clea had seen that look in the eyes of so many men; it had been on Simon Blake's face on the first day he met her. 'You could make an old sack look like a Parisian design.'

And I'll bet you say that to every woman you meet, Clea thought privately, irritation at his blatantly sensual appreciation combining with wry satisfaction at the contrast between Matt's compliments and the way he had described her the last time she had seen him to make it difficult to keep her expression calm and smiling as he spoke again.

'You don't have a drink. Let me——'

He raised a hand and as if from nowhere a waiter appeared with a tray of glasses. Clea accepted the white wine offered her with a careful smile, fully expecting that, his formal duty done, Matt would now move on, already Stan Bowen and the others had melted into the crowd. To her surprise he appeared inclined to linger.

'So tell me, what do you think of the Argyle?'

'On the whole I like what I've seen—though that isn't very much—just the main hall and this dining-room.'

There was a faint breathless note in Clea's voice. She had only just realised how, without her being aware of it, Matt had manoeuvred himself into a position between her and the other models, his powerful frame cutting her off from her friends completely. Just for a second she felt once again that fluttering sensation in the pit of her stomach, and she took a sip of her wine to ease the feeling.

'Perhaps you'd like to see the rest of the place?'

Not with you, thank you very much, Clea was tempted to retort, but such an answer would betray her feelings to him, might make him suspect they had met before, so she schooled her expression into one of polite interest.

'I'd be interested to see what sort of facilities you provide.' It was impossible to resist the temptation to let a deliberately provocative note slide into her voice. 'I've often found that hotel rooms are perfectly adequate for men, but if you want to cater for women on their own—businesswomen and the like—you have to provide a few extras that will appeal to them.'

'Indeed?' Straight dark brows drew together for a moment in a thoughtful expression. 'Well, perhaps you'll give me your opinion of what we provide here.'

Before she quite realised what he intended her glass was taken firmly from her grip and placed on a nearby table, then a hand slid under her elbow, turning her and directing her towards the door.

'Now?' Clea was unable to hide her amazement. Dark grey eyes regarded her with a hint of amusement and she was thoroughly disconcerted to see that under the smile that crossed his face lay a deliberate challenge.

'Can you think of a better time?'

'But—won't you be missed?'

Matt's shrug dismissed the noisy party as unimportant.

'I've done my duty—I've been polite to everyone who matters. I reckon I'm entitled to a little time to myself. And besides, Jensen, the manager, is more than capable of handling things here—I wouldn't have appointed him if he wasn't.'

The touch of arrogance in that last remark was only too familiar. Even at twenty-five, when she had first met him, Matt Highland had possessed a self-assurance that had made her feel gauche and naïve in contrast. For a moment Clea hesitated, tension tightening her muscles. Did she want to be alone with this man? It wasn't part of her plan. All she had wanted was to see his reaction to her, his unprepared, instinctive response, unaware of the fact that he had ever seen her before—and that had been quite satisfactory.

A faint, cynical smile crossed Clea's lips as she recalled the way Matt had looked at her, the sensually appreciative smile—— Oh yes, he had seen her as something very different from the awkward, uncertain adolescent he had dismissed so callously all those years ago.

'So—are you coming?'

The smile faded, replaced by a tiny frown of uncertainty as Clea realised with a sense of shock that Matt's reaction was not enough. It in no way soothed the sting of those long-ago memories; if anything it had aggravated the hurt, tearing open the scar that had formed over the wound he had inflicted, leaving it rawly painful once again. She had told herself that just to impress him would be enough, and without vanity she knew she had done just that, but now——

She glanced swiftly at the tall, dark-haired man at her side, the strong-boned face revealing nothing but resigned patience as he waited for her answer, and to her complete consternation she felt anger boiling up inside her like red-hot lava in a volcano so that she had to struggle to stop it pouring out in furious words. Born with more than his fair share of good looks, Matt Highland knew nothing of the uncertainty, the insecurity of someone not blessed with his advantages trying to make their way in a world that judged so much by appearances, and he was just like all the others, like almost every man she had ever met, attracted only by a pretty face, a trim figure, incapable of seeing below the surface, oblivious to the *person* inside the body, a person with feelings that could be hurt. If only there was some way she could show him——A tiny germ of an idea took root in her mind, her mouth firmed and she turned a cool green gaze on Matt.

'Yes, I'm coming, Mr Highland.'

After the noise and heat of the dining-room, the reception area was delightfully cool and peaceful, and Clea paused thankfully, taking long, deep breaths of the fresher, smoke-free air as Matt moved behind the reception desk and surveyed the rows of keys hanging on the wall.

'Which room?' he asked. 'Choose a number.'

Clea considered for a moment, then, 'Seventeen,' she said decisively, and as Matt turned to select the key allowed herself a private, wry smile at the thought that he wouldn't guess the reason for her choice of that particular number. She had been seventeen nine years ago; seventeen, still at school, and painfully self-conscious and shy—and Matt Highland had taken her vulnerable, fragile ego and trampled it underfoot with one callous remark.

'Seventeen it is.'

As Matt came from behind the desk, the key ring hooked over one finger, the doorman, attracted by the movement and voices in the foyer, came through the door, an enquiring look on his face. Then, clearly recognising Matt, he lifted a hand in smart salute.

'Can I be of any assistance, sir?'

'No, thanks, Dan,' Matt answered offhandedly. 'I'm just showing Miss Mallory round the place.'

Did he know the name of every employee? Clea wondered as she followed him in the direction of the lift. It was unlikely that he had ever seen the doorman before tonight, the hiring of employees to fill such menial posts would surely have been left to the Argyle's manager, and yet he was already on first-name terms with him. He must have a phenomenal memory.

That thought brought a sensation like the cold prick of pins and needles in her veins. What if Matt remembered that summer of nine years ago? No, she reassured herself hastily, if he had she would have seen some sign of it in his face—and she had been so very different then. Unconsciously she ran a hand over the smooth, gleaming silk of her hair, its sleek style nothing like the wild, frizzed mane she had thought so sophisticated at seventeen, her eyes going to Matt's face so that she caught the brief frown that darkened it as the lift doors slid shut.

What had brought that frown to his face? she wondered, the sudden lurching of her stomach having no connection with the lift's smooth motion upwards. In the confined space of the small compartment Matt seemed bigger than ever, over-poweringly so, in spite of the extra inches her high heels added to her own five feet ten. His dark hair, only a couple of shades lighter than her own, gleamed in the fluorescent light, and she caught a waft of some musky aftershave which combined with the more potently masculine scent of his body to set her nerves quivering so that she was intensely grateful for the fact that they were only going up one floor and no further. Determined not to meet those deep grey eyes for fear he might read her reaction in them, she fixed her gaze directly on the black bow of his tie and waited for the lift to stop.

'Here we are.'

Matt stood back to let her precede him and she stepped out into a silent, thickly carpeted corridor, anonymous and soulless as all hotel corridors everywhere. Unhesitatingly Matt led her to a door marked with the number seventeen.

After the restrained elegance of the main foyer and dining-room, Clea had anticipated that the Argyle's bedrooms would be attractive and comfortable, and this one did not disappoint her. Large windows would make it light and airy in the daytime, a comfortable-looking settee and two chairs were ranged near a brand-new television set, a double wardrobe and a dressing-table ran down one wall and the bed, which was kingsize, was covered in a heavy brocade bedspread in soft pinks and turquoise, colours which were taken up in the matching curtains and the carpet.

'Well?'

'Very nice.'

Clea kept her tone neutral with an effort. She was suddenly

painfully conscious of the fact that she was alone with this man
in the intimate surroundings of a bedroom—even if it was only
a hotel room. Everything was very still and quiet, the sounds
of the city's traffic outside hushed by efficient double glazing
and the noise and music of the party only one floor below no
longer audible.

'I'd like to look around, if I may.'

The faint lift of one dark eyebrow sent a flash of anger
through her. Matt Highland clearly did not believe that she
had come up here to see the room but that she had used the
idea simply as an excuse to be alone with him. Her hand itched
to wipe that expression of ironic scepticism from his handsome
face, but Matt forestalled her action by murmuring smoothly,
'Be my guest.'

He lounged back against the wall, his arms folded across his
broad chest, that look of resignation once more on his face. All
right, we'll play the game your way, his expression said. If you
want to keep up the pretence a while longer I don't mind, I can
wait.

You can wait till hell freezes over, Mr Highland! Clea told
him in the privacy of her own thoughts. It would give her
great pleasure to prolong her inspection of the room as long as
she could, and she felt a cynical satisfaction at the knowledge
that his dark eyes, now touched with frank disbelief, followed
every move she made as she opened drawers, looked into the
wardrobe, and finally made her way into the en-suite bathroom
adjoining the bedroom.

Automatically she noted the small touches that lifted this
room out of the class of merely functional and into that of
comfort. Soft towelling robes in the same turquoise as the thick
towels hung on the back of the bathroom door, sachets of
shampoo, conditioner and bath gel, together with packets
containing disposable shower caps, were arranged in a wicker

basket beside the handbasin. Slowly Clea wandered back into the bedroom, her gaze going slowly round it, seeing the boxes of tissues, the provision of a kettle and all that was needed to make a cup of tea or coffee—there were even a couple of small bottles of Perrier water on the desk, which also bore a folder of notepaper and envelopes stamped with the Highland Hotels motif. At last she gave a small nod of approval.

'You've thought of almost everything.'

'*Almost* everything?' echoed Matt, a questioning note lifting his voice. With an effort Clea swallowed down a smile of triumph. He hadn't expected her to take this quite so seriously.

'What about a hairdryer—or an electric razor for a man?'

'Both available from the housekeeper—as is an ironing service—they've only got to ask. Satisfied?'

She was more than satisfied, in fact she was impressed, but she had no intention of showing it. A touch of satirical amusement in Matt's tone caught on her nerves. He still believed her inspection of the room was only a front, a way of playing hard to get for a while, and she was determined to disillusion him on that point. Perversely, having admitted to herself that the room was exactly in keeping with the Highland motto, both comfortable and efficient, she now wanted to find some fault with it.

'I'd like to see a few more coathangers—hotels never seem to provide enough. There should be proper skirt and trouser hangers too.'

'I'll get that seen to.'

There was no amusement in Matt's voice now, it was firm and decisive, and Clea had no doubt that he would act on her comments—and very swiftly too, if she was any judge. Very likely instructions would be issued to that effect first thing tomorrow morning. It was impossible not to feel a small sense of triumph at the way he had taken her opinion so seriously, but she sobered abruptly at the thought that Matt would never have listened to her younger self so seriously; he had barely even acknowledged that Patti Donovan existed until he had crushed her with those hard, cruel words. That bitter memory made her voice stiff and proud when she spoke again.

'Well, I've seen all I want to see—now I think it's time we went back to the party.'

Matt straightened up slowly. 'Is that really what you want?'

The note of reluctance in his voice sounded sincere, but those grey eyes questioned the veracity of her statement in a way that infuriated Clea. She had no intention of letting his tone sway her. Matt Highland had always had a smooth, glib tongue, he had been so flatteringly charming—to her face at least. It was only behind her back, when he hadn't known she was listening, that he had actually spoken the truth.

'Don't you think you should be getting back to your guests?' Once more memory sharpened her voice. 'And I shall have to be going——'

'So soon? It's barely ten o'clock.'

'I'm a working girl, Mr Highland, and I need my sleep. If I don't get a full eight hours it shows in my photographs. I'm always in bed by midnight.'

'*Always?*'

What had put that mocking note in his voice once more? A swift glance into those deep grey eyes caught the gleam of amusement and once again one dark eyebrow drifted upwards, implying a question that had her stiffening with indignation.

'Always,' she repeated firmly, adding emphatically,' and *alone.*'

'Did I suggest otherwise?' Matt affected mock innocence.

No, he hadn't *said* anything, but it had been there in his face, in the glint that lightened the darkness of his eyes, just as she had seen it in so many other men—the infuriating assumption that any model was just a pretty face with no brains behind it, a girl who was immediately available to anyone—— Well, not this model, Mr Highland!

'I would like to go back downstairs,' she said, keeping her temper under control with a struggle. 'Thank you for showing me the room, Mr Highland.'

'It was my pleasure,' was the smoothly drawled response. 'And the name's Matt.'

I *know*. The words almost slipped out and she had to bite down hard on her lower lip to stop them escaping. If only he knew just how well aware of his name she was—and had been for some months even before the first time she had met him. Barry's conversation had been peppered with 'Matt this' and 'Matt that' until Clea had felt that when the famed Matt Highland finally arrived the reality was bound to be a letdown. But it hadn't been, Matt had affected her life with the force of a nuclear explosion, turning it upside down in the space of a few short hours and she had never been the same again.

Matt had moved now, coming to her side, so close that Clea felt he must surely see the involuntary stiffening of her tall, slender body and hear the sudden pounding of her heart. With a smile that stunned her with its devastating charm he lifted one hand and trailed the backs of his fingers lightly down the side of her face, and for all his touch was so gentle Clea felt it as intensely as a searing burn and started away jerkily. Matt's smile didn't waver and he dropped his hand on to her shoulder, curving over her delicate bones, the warmth of his palm reaching her through the fine material of her jacket.

'Do we have to go back downstairs?' he murmured huskily. The seductive note in his voice might have swayed a more gullible woman quite easily, but Clea had long since been cured of believing in Matt Highland or taking him at face-value. 'I thought we could have our own private party——'

Now we're getting to the truth, she thought, the real reason why he brought me up here, and, remembering the look that had been on his face a few minutes earlier, she was once more seized with a longing to feel the impact of her palm against that handsome, smiling face.

'Up here?' Clea's voice was high and sharp and, as he heard it, a faint frown crossed Matt's face but disappeared swiftly as he gave a careless shrug.

'Wherever you like. I could take you home if you preferred, or——'

Clea did not let him finish. 'I'd much rather go back to the party. My friends will be wondering where I've got to.'

The gleam of mockery was back in Matt's eyes once more. 'Do you have to report all your comings and goings to them?' he asked on a note of irony that had Clea drawing herself up to her full height, her eyes bright with irritation.

'I don't *have* to! It's a matter of courtesy—I came with them.' And I have every intention of going home with them, she added silently to herself.

Matt's hand still lingered on her shoulder and it was all she could do not to twist sharply away from his touch. This was not at all how she had planned things—but then she hadn't really formed any coherent plan, the only thought in her mind being to arouse Matt's interest, make him see her as someone very different from the seventeen-year-old Patti Donovan he had treated with such scorn. Well, she'd done that all right, but it seemed he was far more interested than she had ever anticipated, and from his response to her none too subtle attempts to be off-putting he clearly didn't intend to take no for an answer.

'Why are you so keen to get back to that damn party?' For

the first time annoyance had crept into Matt's voice, and Clea felt a small glow of triumph at having ruffled that confident, imperturbable calm at last. 'I could have sworn you weren't enjoying it any more than I was.'

So he had seen her unease; seen it and, thank goodness, misinterpreted the reasons for it.

'It's a public function—part of the job. I really should—'

Clea stopped short, frozen into silence by the look in Matt's eyes. That dark grey gaze was intent on her face, she could feel her skin burn with colour where it rested, and the gleam in his eyes left her in no doubt about his intentions. He was going to kiss her. Tension gripped her, her lips going suddenly dry, and as she wetted them nervously with her tongue she saw his eyes drop to follow the small betraying movement.

Immediately she pulled herself together. This was nothing new. She'd been in this situation many times before and knew how to handle it. That younger Clea might have panicked, blurting out some foolish protest, but she was no longer seventeen. As Matt's head lowered slowly she moved away, carefully, smoothly, with just a slight twist to her head so that his mouth brushed over her hair instead of making contact with her lips as he had intended. She prided herself on the fact that her action looked completely natural, as if she had moved quite spontaneously without any awareness of his intention or any plan of avoiding his kiss.

In the doorway Clea turned to look back at the man standing in the middle of the room, the darkness of his hair and his black evening clothes seeming suddenly alien and strangely threatening in contrast to the soft colours of the room's décor. Was it anger that had turned his narrowed eyes black and hard as jet? She couldn't tell, and the rest of his face gave nothing away. Clea met that cool, considering look directly, her own eyes widening with a hint of defiance.

'I think it's time we rejoined the party,' she said calmly before she walked out of the room without a backward glance, leaving him with no alternative but to follow her.

Matt caught her up as she pressed the button to summon the lift, his hand closing over hers, twisting her round, and before she had time to protest she was pulled close up against the hard strength of his body, the dark head lowered swiftly and her lips were captured in a crushing, bruising kiss, the force of which sent her senses reeling so that for a second she was powerless to resist. But that second was long enough for Matt to do exactly as he wanted, to take the kiss she had thwarted him of before, and as the lift arrived, its doors sliding open as it came to a halt beside them, he released her, standing back with an expression of smiling triumph on his face as he made a small, mocking bow with a gesture to indicate that she should precede him into the lift.

Still too stunned to speak, Clea stalked past him, thoroughly disconcerted to find that her legs were not quite steady beneath her. Her green eyes flashed fire as they met Matt's grey ones, but that simply broadened the smile on his face, turning it into a wicked, taunting grin.

'*Now* we'll rejoin the party,' he said quietly, but there was a note in his voice that brought hot colour rushing up into Clea's face and kept her rigid, her body held stiffly away from his, as she stood in stony silence while the lift began to descend.

CHAPTER TWO

THE TAXI drew up outside the hotel and Dan the doorman stepped forward to open the door, an umbrella held aloft against the driving rain that had started to fall just as the party ended. Under its protection Penny, Claire and Althea crossed the pavement and got into the waiting car. Clea was just about to follow them when a tall, masculine figure appeared from the brightly lit foyer and a large hand caught hold of her arm in a grip that was just strong enough to prevent any movement.

'I'll see Miss Mallory home, Dan,' Matt Highland said firmly.

Oh no, you won't! The words boiled up inside her, but she swallowed them down hastily. She had no intention of causing a scene on the steps of the Argyle with all the guests at the party well within earshot as they waited for their cars to be brought round.

'I'd prefer to go with my friends,' she began, but her words were drowned by the slam of the taxi door and the roar of its engine. Clearly Dan knew which side his bread was buttered and he had no intention of crossing his employer.

Her face pale with suppressed anger, Clea watched the taxi pull away. In the light of the street lamps she could see Penny's small face staring back at her, her eyes wide with unconcealed curiosity. She would have to face a barrage of questions tomorrow, she thought wryly. As the taxi turned the corner out of sight she swung round, meeting the cool, dark eyes of the man at her side with open defiance.

'I didn't need a lift home, Mr Highland,' she said tautly.

'Your Mr Bowen had made arrangements——'

'And I'm unmaking them,' Matt parried smoothly. 'I think you'll be more comfortable in my car instead of being crammed into a taxi with three others. Besides,' he went on as she opened her mouth to protest further, 'you live on the opposite side of town to the other girls. You'll get home much more quickly if you come with me.'

Clea's open lips closed and tightened. How did he know that? Stan Bowen knew where she lived; he had sent the taxi that had collected her and brought her here this evening. But he was unlikely to have offered that information casually, which could only mean that Matt had asked him directly, a thought that had her huddling deeper into her fur jacket with a shiver that had nothing to do with the chill that the rain had brought to the evening.

In the minute that the lift doors had opened as they reached the ground floor she had made her escape, hurrying into the brightly lit dining-room without a backward glance, only relaxing when she was swallowed up in the crowd, hidden from Matt Highland's keen dark eyes. For the rest of the evening she had avoided him carefully, sticking close to the other three models and watching the clock, anxious for the moment when they could leave. She had hoped to disappear without coming face to face with Matt again, but his sudden appearance at the door of the hotel had ruined that plan.

'This is my car,' said Matt as a sleek black Jaguar driven by one of the hotel's employees drew up beside them. He moved to open the passenger door and stood back, waiting.

For a second Clea hesitated. She had no wish to be alone in the car with this man—but it appeared she had no choice. She was none too sure what his reaction would be if she flatly refused to get into the car, but she rather suspected it would be something she had better not risk. Already several of the other guests were casting frankly curious glances her way. *Damm you,* Matt Highland! Clea thought furiously as, with her head held stiffly erect, she moved forward.

'It's a foul night,' Matt commented smoothly as he steered the car out into the dark street, its windscreen wipers struggling against the lashing rain. 'Not many women would refuse a lift home in this weather.'

'I've already told you I had transport arranged.'

'But, as *I* told *you,* its much more convenient if I take you.' Dark eyes slid to Clea's face in a swift, sidelong glance. 'I'm not a rapist, Miss Mallory, nor am I about to abduct you and sell you to the white slave trade—so why not sit back and enjoy the journey?'

The hint of mockery in his voice made her painfully aware of the way she was sitting stiffly in her seat, her small evening bag clutched tightly in her hands. With an effort she made herself lean back, uncomfortably conscious of the way the movement brought her nearer to Matt's broad shoulders, his hand disturbingly close to her leg as he changed gear smoothly.

'You're not the sort of man who can take a hint, are you?' she said sharply, and heard his muffled snort of laughter.

'Oh, I can take a hint all right—but sometimes it suits me better to ignore it.'

'And tonight is one of those times?'

'That's right,' Matt agreed imperturbably.

'Do you mind if I ask why?'

'Not at all—but I'm sure you can guess.'

'I have no idea what you mean.'

Matt laughed again. 'Oh, come now, Clea—you're a very beautiful woman and you know it. You wouldn't be in your job if you didn't. And you're no innocent fresh from the schoolroom, you must know when a man's interested.'

'And you are—interested?' A sudden dryness in Clea's mouth, a stiffness in her throat, made the words come out tightly.

Another of those keen, sidelong glances flickered over her face. 'What do you think?'

'I think you're an arrogant, self-centred male who can't take no for an answer,' Clea declared squashingly.

But Matt was not at all squashed. 'Not can't, Clea,' he corrected drily. 'I could if I wanted to, but I've no intention of doing so. I want to get to know you.'

A sudden silence descended as she absorbed that remark. Things were moving rather too fast for her and she was not at all sure she liked the way they were going. She had planned on showing Matt she was a very different person from the girl he had scorned in the past, and from the moment she had seen that spark of appreciation in his eyes she had succeeded—but she hadn't bargained on him being quite *this* interested.

'And what if I don't want to get to know you?'

I don't need to get to know you, she added in her thoughts. I know all I need to already—know you and don't like you.

'That's a very hasty judgement,' Matt returned blandly. 'Have I been rude—done anything to offend you?'

You kissed me. Clea wanted to cry, but swallowed the words down hastily. It wasn't the kiss that had upset her, she'd been kissed often enough by men she didn't particularly like and it hadn't shaken her in the way Matt's kiss had. She had been furious at the effrontery of his action, his arrogant taking of what he wanted and to hell with the consequences, but since then she'd had time to think and had been forced to admit that what had really angered her was the fact that he had wanted to kiss Clea Mallory when he would never have considered kissing Patti Donovan, a bitter taste filling her mouth as she recalled the nights she had dreamed of such a kiss, creating a fantasy that had been so very different from the reality. Matt's action had confirmed her suspicion that, like all men, he was attracted only by the surface glamour, and for that she despised him.

'Look,' she tried hard to keep her voice calm and reasonable, 'can't you just accept that I'm not as attracted to you as you are to me? It happens all the time.'

'If you can give me one good reason for your opinion I'll consider it.'

Give him a reason! Clea's head whirled as she tried to think. There was no explanation she could offer other than the fact that she was Patti Donovan—or, rather, had been when he had known her, and for reasons that weren't quite clear, even to herself, she didn't want him to know that yet.

'Look,' Matt was saying, 'all I'm asking is that you see me again. One evening spent together—is that so very much to ask?'

'No.' The word had formed before Clea had time to think if it was wise or not. It implied a concession, a weakening of her resolve, and she had no intention of giving in. But even as she told herself that, another idea was taking root in her mind. Earlier in the evening she had admitted that simply to have Matt Highland interested in her was not enough. Deep inside her she still sensed the remembered pain of the seventeen-year-old Patti, felt again the savage destruction of her fragile self-confidence, and a bitter anger filled her mind.

Her green eyes swung to the man at her side, resting on his handsome face seen in flashes as they passed the street lamps. He was so sure of himself, so smugly arrogant. She'd dearly love to puncture that inflated self-esteem, bring him down a peg or two—and he had given her the perfect opening.

'Here we are, Cinderella. You're home—and it's still half an hour till midnight.'

Clea looked about her in flustered surprise. Absorbed in her thoughts, she hadn't been aware of the fact that they had reached the street in which she lived. As the car drew up outside the house in which she had the upstairs flat she realised that the time had come to make up her mind. She had to decide one way or another—but which was it to be? Matt switched off the engine and turned to face her, his eyes very deep and dark in his shadowed face.

'Clea——' he began, and his use of her name jolted her into action. She had not given him permission to use it, had done nothing that would ever make him think she encouraged such familiarity, and yet he had spoken her name with an ease that suggested they were friends—or more. It was typical of his arrogance to assume that because he was who he was, because he was, in theory at least, the tall, dark and handsome man of most women's dreams, she must inevitably be attracted to him. Well, she would take great pleasure in pulling that particular rug from under his feet.

'One evening, you said?' she said carefully, making it sound as if she was reconsidering, as if all she needed was a little more persuasion, and, from the gleam in his eyes, that was exactly what Matt thought. He probably believed her initial reaction was simply playing hard to get, she reflected cynically.

'I thought we could have dinner together after the fashion show tomorrow. Will you be free then?'

'Yes, I'll be free.'

The words came slowly, Clea was still considering the matter. Could she go through with this? Did she want to? Another swift glance at that strong-boned face, remembered so long from the dreams of her adolescence—dreams he had shattered with a few careless words—convinced her. She would enjoy bringing Matt Highland down from the pedestal on which he had put himself. He probably thought no woman could resist him. Well, she'd make him think again.

What had he called her? Cinderella? Perhaps it fitted in a way—she had certainly been transformed from the Patti he had known, just as Cinderella had been changed by the power of her fairy godmother. But there had been no wicked stepmother or stepsisters, just a stepfather whom no one could describe as wicked. Ned had always been kindness itself, and Barry—— But Matt was still waiting for an answer.

'All right,' Clea said slowly. 'Dinner tomorrow.'

That devastating smile flashed over his face. 'I'll be at the show, so I'll collect you after it—say nine-thirty?'

'That'll suit me. And now I really must go.'

As Clea pressed the button that released her seat-belt Matt leaned forward, his face coming directly into the light of the street lamp, his intent as easily readable as it had been in the hotel room a short time before. Hastily Clea moved back out of reach, proffering her hand.

'Goodnight, Mr Highland,' she said firmly. 'I'll see you tomorrow.'

Matt's firm mouth tightened perceptibly and Clea had to steel herself to meet his eyes as they narrowed assessingly. She had meant to make a point and he knew it—and from the look on his face he was none too pleased about it. But he reached out and took her hand calmly enough.

'Goodnight, Clea,' he said softly, then confounded her completely by turning her hand in his own and pressing a firm, warm kiss on the backs of her fingers. 'Until tomorrow,' he murmured, his tone leaving her unclear as to whether the words were a promise or a threat. 'Oh, and Clea——' he added as she got out out of the car, 'the name's Matt, remember.'

Remember! How could I ever forget! Clea was tempted to shout the words after the car as it moved off down the road. She hadn't forgotten his name in nine long years, she was hardly likely to do so now.

The next day was a Saturday and apart from the fashion show at the Argyle that evening Clea had no commitments. Normally that would have meant that she could allow herself the luxury of an all too rare lie-in, but this particular morning sleep eluded her. She felt restless and ill at ease, and from the moment her eyes opened to a clear bright morning with no sign of the rainstorm that had lashed her windows far into the night she felt she had to get up and find something to do. The hours before six o'clock when she was due at the Argyle, where she could submerge her restless feelings in the bustle and activity of preparing for the fashion show, stretched ahead like a dry, arid desert with nothing to break up the monotonous stretch of time.

Coming to a decision, Clea flung back the bedclothes and swung her feet out of the bed. A few minutes later, clad in a pink and blue leotard, she went into her small living-room, pushed back the settee and chairs, then selected a tape which she slipped into her cassette player. For the next hour she subjected herself to a rigorous workout, bending, stretching, twisting, using every muscle to its fullest ability, driving herself harder than she had ever done, even in those early days when her determination to lose weight had been the driving force behind her actions. When the tape finished she turned it over and started again, coming to a halt only when she heard a knock at her door. She knew who it would be without having to ask.

'Come in, Maggie!' she called, her voice only very faintly breathless after her exertions. 'The door's not locked.'

She smiled a welcome as her neighbour came into the room. Maggie Fletcher who, at thirty-one, was five years older than Clea had been her friend ever since she had moved into the downstairs flat four years before. Meeting her in the hall one evening, Clea had invited her in for coffee and the two women had taken an instant liking to each other, one that had grown into a warm friendship that had deepened with the years.

'Working out—at this time on a Saturday!' Maggie exclaimed. 'Clea, honey, you're a fanatic!'

'I didn't disturb you, did I?' asked Clea in some concern, moving to switch off the cassette player.

Maggie shook her head, sending her mane of flame-red hair flying.

'No chance of that, love. I was wining and dining last night and I didn't get to bed until two. You could have knocked the house down round my ears and I wouldn't have woken. I've only just surfaced.'

'Have you had breakfast? I could——'

'Not for me, thanks,' Maggie put in. 'I ate some sinfully calorie-laden food last night, so today will have to be a penance day to make up for it.' With a rueful smile she glanced down at her statuesque figure, then her eyes went to Clea's slim waist and hips in the clinging leotard. 'It's all right for you, you can eat what you like and get away with it.'

Clea's smile slipped slightly. 'Now, Maggie, you know that isn't true. You've seen the evidence.'

Instinctively her head turned towards the kitchen, her gaze going to the larder door, Maggie stuck pictures of beautiful, slender women all over her fridge and food cupboard to remind her of the way she wanted to look, but Clea knew exactly how she wanted to be, it was what she had been that she needed to recall. One glance at the photograph of herself aged seventeen pinned up on the inside of the larder door was enough to crush any temptation to indulge and keep her firmly on the straight and narrow.

'Oh, come off it, Clea!' Maggie expostulated. 'You haven't

looked like that for years and you know it.'

Maybe she did, but the memory still lurked at the back of her mind like some overly-substantial ghost, and last night's meeting with Matt Highland had ruined her chances of laying that ghost once and for all.

'But I didn't come to talk about diets——'

Something quivered in the pit of Clea's stomach as she anticipated her friend's next remark.

'I'm dying to know how you got on last night. Did you meet the infamous Matt Highland?' The gleam in Maggie eyes intensified at Clea's nod. 'And what happened?'

Clea hesitated, then decided to come clean. Maggie would know if she didn't tell the truth.

'I'm having dinner with him tonight.'

Maggie's response was a long, low whistle of astonishment.

'You're doing what? But I thought the idea was——'

'I know what I planned,' Clea put in hastily. 'But it didn't work out like that.'

How could she explain just what it had been like? She had spent most of the time before she had finally fallen asleep wondering how she had let herself be manoeuvred into seeing Matt again, and she still couldn't quite believe that it had happened.

'Was he still the way you remember him?'

'Just the same.' Clea's mouth tightened. 'Just as good-looking and every bit as arrogant and self-centred as he ever was.'

'Then why are you seeing him again?'

With a sigh Clea pushed a slender hand through the blue-black silk of her hair.

'I'm not really sure. I meant to do just as I said—I just wanted him to notice me, see me as something very different from the teenager I was when I first met him—but then I found that wasn't enough. He hurt me, Maggie, and I wanted to hurt him too—let him know what it feels like to be crushed so completely you think you'll never recover.'

'So what are you going to do?'

Clea's smile was hard. 'I'm going to date him a few times—get him keen but keep him dangling on a string. Then, when I'm ready, I'll drop him . . .' Her voice trailed off as she met her friend's eyes. 'You don't approve?'

'It's not for me to approve or disapprove, love. I can understand your feelings. You've told me that Matt Highland behaved like a bastard with a capital B, but it was all so long ago. Is it worth raking it all up again?'

For a moment Clea hesitated, acknowledging the truth of what Maggie had said. It had all been a long time ago, but last night had brought it all back, making her feel as vulnerable as the teenager who had first met Matt Highland, the veneer of self-confidence she had acquired over the years stripped way in a few short hours. An image of Matt's darkly handsome face floated before her mind's eye and she saw again the deliberately assessing glance that had swept over her, the sensual gleam that had lightened those deep grey eyes. She had seen that look too often in the eyes of other men, men like Simon Blake who saw women merely as decorative playthings to be used and then abandoned.

'It's not just the past, Maggie, it's now—the way he behaved last night. He's another Simon.'

'Ah!' Maggie needed no further explanation. She knew the story of Simon Blake and all the others who, attracted by the superficial allure of Clea's job as a model, had sought her out, thinking she was an easy target, only to discard her coldly, without a second thought, when she had made it clear that she didn't intend to jump straight into bed with them. 'But you can't blame Matt Highland for the way Simon treated you.'

'No—but knowing Simon meant that I can recognise his type when I see it—and Matt Highland's Simon Blake all over again. I was too young to know how to handle Simon and he hurt me very badly—but things are very different now.' And Matt Highland was going to find out just how different things were.

'You're determined to go through with this, then?'

Clea nodded firmly, her fine-boned face hardening. 'Men of that sort use us as objects, Maggs. We're nothing but an attractive face and a good body to them. You should know that,' she added, referring to Maggie's divorce which had been the reason for the older woman moving into the downstairs flat originally, 'Doug was just the same. All I'm going to do is to turn the tables on one of them for a change—use Matt Highland as he'd like to use me.'

'It's your decision, kiddo.' Maggie's face was serious. 'But be careful. Revenge has a nasty way of going sour. It can turn round and hurt you when you least expect it.

CHAPTER THREE

'REVENGE has a nasty way of going sour.' Maggie's words echoed over and over in Clea's head as she submitted to the ministrations of the hairdresser and make-up artist before the fashion show that evening. She would have preferred to do her own make-up, she was perfectly capable of doing a professional job, and the small, practical tasks would have occupied her mind, kept her from thinking of the evening ahead of her at the end of the show, about which she was having very strong second thoughts.

Determinedly pushing her uneasy thoughts to the back of her mind, she headed for the long rail that held the clothes she was to model, all carefully arranged in the correct order. From the moment her hand rested on the first outfit she was caught up in the well-known routine, the constant changes of clothes, the need for split-second timing combining to prevent her from thinking of anything other than the job in hand. The sound of disco music filled her head and automatically her slender body moved in time to the beat. She was a professional and she was going to give the performance of her life.

The routine came as naturally to her as breathing. She moved down the catwalk with graceful strides, her head held erect, her face aloof, no smile curving her lips. She knew her job, she was just a moving coathanger—it was the clothes the audience had come to see, not the model.

It was half-way through the show that she first saw Matt. He was leaning against the wall in a corner of the room, immaculate in a tailored dark blue suit and paler blue shirt, his arms folded across his broad chest, his dark eyes fixed on her with an intensity that made her feel he could see straight through the elegant clothes, strip away the careful make-up and see the young Patti Donovan buried deep inside her.

For a second her footsteps faltered. She hesitated, almost missed the beat, but then swiftly recovered. Her head lifted a fraction, giving her a haughty, aristocratic look, every trace of nervousness hidden under a carefully smooth mask. Patti no longer existed; let Matt see the real Clea!

For the rest of the evening she carefully avoided looking in the direction of Matt's tall, powerful figure, but all the time she was supremely conscious of his silent, watchful presence, and when she made her final appearance in a scarlet silk sheath with a daringly split skirt she imagined she could feel his eyes resting on the exposed flesh of her arms and shoulders, her skin burning at the thought.

And then the show was over, the music died away, and Clea sank into a chair with a sigh of relief.

'Where's Clea?' The make-up artist's voice reached her across the room. 'Oh, there you are. I've a message for you. Matthew Highland came to see you, but I told him you hadn't changed yet. He asked me to tell you that he'll wait for you in the bar.'

'Thanks, Janice.' Clea's acknowledgement was abstracted. The time had come to face the decision she knew she had been avoiding all evening. Was she going through with this or not?

Her mind still wasn't completely made up as she crossed the reception hall on her way to the bar some time later, her footsteps slowing as she neared the glass doors and finally came to a halt as she caught sight of an all too familiar figure just a few yards away from her, his back towards her so that he was unaware of her presence as she considered him thoughtfully. It would be a simple matter to find a porter, ask him to pass on the message that she had changed her mind and wouldn't be coming after all. But that was sheer cowardice, the sort of craven behaviour she might have expected from Patti. Clea was made of different stuff; she owed it to herself to tell him to his face at least.

But still she could not make her feet move, take the few steps into the bar and up to Matt's side. Her eyes lingered on his tall frame, objectively noting the width of his shoulders under the superbly tailored jacket, the length of his legs, the silken fall of his thick dark hair. When she was seventeen his physical attraction had been potent enough to reduce her legs to jelly, her mind to an unthinking blur, but she had very soon learned that, however attractive the wrapping, the contents of this particular parcel were not at all to her liking.

Suddenly it was as if the years had slipped away, her surroundings faded and Clea was once more that seventeen-year-old living quietly at home with her mother and stepfather.

She had been ten years old when her mother, widowed for four years since Clea's father had died of a heart attack at the early age of forty-two, had met and fallen in love with Edward Donovan, himself a widower with a son seven years older than Clea. There had been few problems adjusting to her new family, Ned had been kindness itself and eventually, with Clea's full agreement, he had adopted her as his own daughter, and his son, Barry, soon became the older brother she had always wished she could have, good-humoured and surprisingly tolerant of the ten-year-old who trailed round after him, lost in a haze of hero-worship that drove her to become something of a tomboy in her determined efforts to keep up with the activities of her stepbrother and his friends.

It had been Barry who had coined the nickname Patti, deriving it from a teasing mockery of her given name which he considered too fancy for the tousle-haired, grubby-kneed ragamuffin she had been. At first he had exaggerated her name to Cleopatra, pronounced with gentle mockery, but soon softened that to the affectionate Patti, a name which had delighted Clea so much that she had insisted that all her family used it. At home she was still called Patti even though she had reverted to the name Clea Mallory when she had first become a model.

It was when she was sixteen that Matthew Highland's name had first been mentioned. Barry, now working in London, had met Matt at a party and the two men had taken to each other from the start. On his frequent visits home Barry was full of stories of his new friend and the renovation and redecoration of the then slightly shabby hotels that comprised the Highland chain he had inherited from his father, and it was inevitable that eventually Ned and Clea's mother should suggest that he bring Matt with him the next time he came home.

Clea had a vivid memory of the first time she had seen Matt's darkly handsome face in a collection of photographs Barry had brought with him.

'There's Matt,' he had said casually, indicating the tall figure of his friend with a pointing finger. 'What do you think of him, then, Patti?'

Clea had simply stared, unable to believe her eyes. At seventeen she was emerging from her tomboy phase into a new awareness of the fact that she was female and was beginning to appreciate the attractions of the opposite sex. Up until this moment such feelings had been concentrated on the current pop stars, posters of whom decorated her bedroom walls, or a painfully embarrassed crush on one of the older boys in her school, but from the moment she saw the lean planes of Matt's handsome face, the powerful body dressed in hip-hugging denim jeans and a clinging T-shirt, such innocent feelings faded before a rush of her first true sexual awareness. Matt Highland was the embodiment of her dreams, a fantasy come true, and she sincerely believed herself in love with him before she had even seen him in the flesh.

That feeling had driven her into a state of blind panic some weeks later when her mother told her that Barry was coming home at the weekend and was bringing Matt Highland home with him. Every night she had dreamed of meeting her fantasy, falling asleep with the photograph of Matt, carefully removed from the folder when Barry wasn't looking, tucked under her pillow. Her dreams had been of the moment they would come face to face, her imagination imprinting an expression of stunned delight on that handsome face, putting a note of shaken awe into the voice she had never heard as Matt said, 'My God, but you're beautiful!' before he gathered her into his arms for a long, passionate kiss. The dream had always ended with that kiss because, although she knew the facts of life, she had no experience that enabled her to translate those facts into emotions. In fact she had never even been kissed, the subjects of her schoolgirl crushes having rejected her attentions with some scornful, derogatory remark about her appearance before they they turned to the prettier, slimmer girls in her class.

Those comments hurt, but Clea couldn't deny their truth, however much she wanted to. It was bad enough being taller than most of the boys in her year, but the problem was compounded by the fact that she was almost two stone overweight, something that had never troubled her when she was younger, when loose trousers and baggy sweaters were her usual weekend wear. But just lately she had wanted to look more like the other girls in her class and had sought out more feminine clothing, only to come up painfully against the fact that the bright, fashionable clothes were made in sizes that only went up to a fourteen. Ned would willingly have bought her a whole wardrobe of new clothes, but the truth was that nothing would fit.

As the day of Matt's arrival drew nearer Clea had sunk deeper into black despair.

'I've got nothing to wear!' she complained to her mother, and Ruth Donovan smiled a gentle reproach.

'Don't be silly, darling,' she said. 'What about your new blue dress?'

Clea scowled darkly. The blue dress, bought in a moment of desperation, was not at all what she had in mind. A loose cotton smock, it looked to her eyes like a vast bell tent, unflattering to say the least, especially since her long black hair had become lank and straight with the onset of adolescence.

'I don't want to wear the blue dress—I want something special—the sort of thing Steph wears.'

As she spoke the other girl's name an idea came to her. Stephanie Peters, who was in her class at school and who lived in the same street, was the sort of girl who always had boys round her like bees round a honeypot. Her clothes were always in the height of fashion and she was rarely seen without make-up; even at school her eyelashes were liberally coated with mascara. On impulse Clea pulled her jacket from its peg in the hall.

'I'm going round to Steph's. I'll be back for tea.'

Saturday morning was sunny and clear and Clea's steps were light as she made her way home. She almost felt like dancing the few hundred yards to the front door, but the high heels on the shoes she had bought secretly the day before hampered her, she found just walking in them difficult enough. Her face felt strange and stiff, her eyelids heavy under their unaccustomed coating of eyeshadow and mascara and the denim skirt, buttoned all the way down the front, that

Steph had given her because it was too big for her dug in unpleasantly at the waistband. But Clea was blind to her discomfort, her thoughts going in delighted anticipation to the meeting ahead of her. She was a little late, Barry's car was already parked by the kerb, but in a way that was all for the best; she would be able to make a dramatic entrance.

'Here's Patti now,' said her mother as she opened the door into the living-room, but Clea barely heard the words, her eyes flying instinctively to the man who had risen from his seat at her entrance. Excitement blurred her vision so that for a moment she had only a confused impression of height and strength and a mane of glossy dark hair.

'Hello, Patti.' The sound of that low-toned voice sent shivers down Clea's spine and she gave herself a little shake, her eyes clearing so that she saw him sharply at last.

She had dreamed of this moment, but the reality was far better than her imaginings. That photograph had only hinted at the forceful impact of Matt's face and those deep grey eyes that were looking straight into hers, slightly narrowed as if he couldn't quite believe what he saw. The direct force of that intent gaze disconcerted her and, suddenly painfully shy, she lowered her eyelids hastily as Matt proffered his hand in greeting, then recollecting herself and remembering that she wanted to appear grown up and sophisticated, she turned the downward glance into a deliberate flutter of her thickly mascaraed lashes, slanting a flirtatious glance at him from her clear green eyes. Her heart lurched, then pounded fiercely at the touch of his hand, and she savoured the warm feel of his fingers against hers for an all too brief moment.

'It's a pleasure to meet you at last,' she said, pitching her voice so that it was low and husky, trying to sound like an actress, she particularly admired, a woman who specialised in playing the *femme fatale*. 'Barry's told us so much about you.'

'And what about me?' Barry's voice broke in on her and he held his arms open wide. 'Come and say hello to your big brother, then. Have you missed me?'

'Of course I have.'

In normal circumstances Clea would have flung herself into those open arms, but, supremely conscious of the other man in the room, she simply gave Barry a swift hug and then moved back hastily, well aware of his penchant for ruffling her hair in a way that did not fit with the image she wanted to present. But Barry was not going to let her get away with that.

'Hey, what's up? Gone off me, have you?' He grabbed her and enfolded her in a hug that drove all the breath from her body, then abruptly released her., his face creasing in a grimace of distaste. 'Pooh! You don't half pong!' was his unflattering response to the perfume she had liberally sprayed all over herself. 'Why are you done up like a dog's dinner? And *what* have you done to your hair?'

'I had it permed,' Clea said in what she hoped was a light and airy tone, though deep inside she was burning with embarrassment at the way her brother was treating her. Ordinarily she would have taken his teasing in good part—but that was when Matt Highland wasn't there. She tossed her tangled mane back over her shoulder in a gesture that she believed was carefree and enticing. The perm had been a last-minute inspiration of Steph's. 'Do you like it?'

The question was directed at Barry, but her eyes went to Matt's face, trying to read his thoughts. She was delighted to see that he was watching her closely, but his narrow-eyed gaze was unfathomable, impossible to interpret.

'It looks as if you got caught in a cyclone,' was Barry's uncomplimentary response, and Clea's hand itched to thump him as she had often done when his teasing got too much.

With difficulty she restrained herself.

'It is a little wild, darling,' her mother's quiet voice put in. 'Where did you have it done?'

'Steph did it for me with a home perm. It was just a spur-of-the-moment idea.' She was pleased with that, it made her sound like a creature of impulse, light-hearted and spontaneous, and from the smile that crossed Matt's face that was exactly how he took it. She flashed a bright smile in his direction.

'Barry says you own some hotels—is that right?'

'Yes, that's true.' Matt's tone was gravely polite. 'They're a bit run-down and old-fashioned, but I have plans to do something about that.'

'Yes, Barry told me you had some great ideas. It sounds so exciting.'

It wasn't difficult to keep a breathless note in her voice. Having Matt's attention centred on her made it difficult to breathe normally and her heart was beating at twice its normal rate so that she felt sure he could hear its heavy pounding.

'Won't you sit down, Patti?' her mother put in, carefully drawing her attention to the fact that Matt was still standing and, following her lead, Clea flashed that brilliant smile at Matt once more.

'Oh yes, do sit down, Matt. We don't stand on ceremony here.'

Matt's response was a gesture of his hand towards the settee. Filled with delight to find that he was too much a gentleman to sit down unless she did, Clea let her smile widen even further, but it faded as she lowered herself on to the settee. The already tight waistband of her skirt dug in even more painfully and the buttons strained noticeably, leaving ugly gaps between them. Steph was some inches shorter than Clea and the skirt which had been outrageously short when she was standing up now seemed practically non-existent, exposing almost all of Clea's long legs encased in black tights—black because Steph had said the colour was slimming.

Clea's heart leapt as Matt came to sit beside her and she turned in her seat so that she was facing him.

'Tell me about your hotels, Matt. I'd like to hear all about your plans for them.'

Later, she was unable to recall a word he had said, she had been too entranced by the sight of him, the warm scent of his long body so close to hers and that attractive deep voice, to take in anything he told her. But what he said didn't matter. He was here, talking to her, their position in the corner of the room excluding everyone else, and if Matt occasionally made a remark to her mother or Ned she would ask another question, lay a hand on his arm to draw his attention back to her.

Excitement went to her head like the effect of some potent wine and she flirted outrageously, using everything she had ever heard of or read about body language to tell Matt how she felt.

'I'd love to live in London,' she said when the subject of the renovation work on the hotels had been exhausted, leaning towards Matt with a flattering display of attention so that he could not be unware of the way her breasts strained against the tight-fitting, low-cut T-shirt she wore. She saw his dark eyes rest on the soft curves and her breath caught in her throat so that she could hardly get the next words out. 'It must be wonderful—so very different from living here.'

'Do you think so?' Matt's tone was dry. 'I rather envy you living in the country myself.'

'Oh, I can't believe that!' Clea exclaimed archly. 'It's terribly boring. There's nothing to do.'

That wasn't exactly true. Clea had plenty of social life and really enjoyed living in the small northern town, but she couldn't believe that a sophisticated Londoner like Matt would find the few parties and occassional discos she went to in the least bit interesting, and she had no wish to appear like a country bumpkin in his eyes.

'Then perhaps you'd like to come and stay with Barry some time. If I'm free I could show you round.'

Oh yes, please! I'd love that! The words almost slipped out in the rush of heady joy that sent a wave of colour into her cheeks. This time her smile was completely natural and totally without artifice, and it drew those grey eyes to her face with an expression that was new and very different, Matt's pupils widening until his eyes looked totally black. But then Clea caught herself up, remembering the sophisticated role she was playing and, belatedly recalling Steph's advice to play it cool, play hard to get, she turned her wide, adolescent grin into a gracious smile.

'That would be nice,' she said coolly. 'If I'm ever in town I might take you up on that.'

She'd slipped up somewhere. Matt's smile had died and a frown darkened his face. Mentally Clea cursed Steph. She'd got it all wrong—men needed to know you were interested; the play it cool bit didn't work. Hastily she set herself to repair the damage.

'Will you be staying with us long?' she asked, her eyes wide and hopeful.

'Just the one night, I'm afraid. I had hoped to make it longer, but something's cropped up and I shall have to get back tomorrow.'

So soon? Clea wanted to cry out in protest. She had only just begun to get to know him. But he had sounded genuinely regretful that his visit was only to be a short one, and that was enough to sustain her through the rest of the afternoon and the evening, time that passed in a haze of delight for Clea. Happiness loosened her tongue so that she positively sparkled at the dinner table, stunning her family who were more used to her rather withdrawn shyness. She kept all her most brilliant smiles, her best witticisms, her languishing glances for Matt, seated directly opposite her, and had the satisfaction of seeing his eyes on her at many points during the meal, so that when she reluctantly retired to bed she felt as if she was floating inches above the floor, her feet not touching the ground. She fell asleep almost as soon as her head touched the pillow, and her dreams were filled with the image of a tall man with shining dark hair and a pair of watchful grey eyes.

In the morning she was up bright and early, sitting before her dressing-table and struggling with the bottles and packs of make-up Stephanie had lent her. It wasn't as easy as the other girl had made it seem, but at last she managed something close to the effect of the day before and she turned her attention to her hair. The perm had been an inspiration, she decided, the riot of curls giving her a wild, gipsyish look that was well worth the torment of trying to drag a comb through the tangled mane. She had almost finished when she heard the sound of voice in the garden, reaching her clearly through her partly-open window.

'I think we should be ready to re-open soon.' It was Matt's voice, she would recognise those deep tones anywhere, it had rung in her ears all night, speaking words of love in her dreams.

Clea hurried to the window and peered out. Matt and her brother were standing just below her, their backs towards the window. Leaning out as far as she dared, she let her eyes wander hungrily over Matt's powerful frame, lingering on the width of his shoulders and chest, the long line of his legs in black cord trousers, and her mouth dried with excitement. She had never really understood the meaning of the word sexy until now, she thought, missing her brother's next comment.

A slight movement of Matt's dark head as if turning towards the window had her shrinking back inside. She didn't want to be caught watching him like this, it was the sort of gauche behaviour she was trying to avoid.

'I'll need new staff, of course, once the alterations are complete,' Matt was saying. 'The place was dreadfully understaffed before—and as if things weren't bad enough the receptionist's just told me she's leaving to have a baby so I'll have her to replace as well.'

'Perhaps you could find a vacancy for Patti somewhere,' Barry put in. 'She's leaving school in the summer and she hasn't an idea of what she's going to do. What about this receptionist's job?'

Clea's heart missed a beat. A job for her—working for Matt Highland in one of his hotels where she was likely to see him very frequently! It would be a dream come true. She closed her eyes, her fingers crossed superstitiously as she waited tensely for Matt's reply.

'A receptionist—Patti?' Matt's laugh was harsh, the cold contempt in his voice searing along Clea's sensitive nerves. 'Have a heart, Barry! I want someone attractive, a good advertisement for the hotel—someone who'll make the guests glad they chose a Highland hotel, not some tarty little Lolita who'll frighten them away.'

CHAPTER FOUR

'EXCUSE ME.'

Clea started, coming back to the present with jolt. She glanced up into the face of the man who had spoken, a wave of colour washing her cheeks as she realised that she was standing directly in his path.

'Oh, I'm sorry! I must have been dreaming!' she murmured, moving aside hastily, her eyes going swiftly to the dark figure beyond the glass doors as she prayed that the small disturbance hadn't alerted Matt to her presence. She wanted to collect her thoughts, regain some degree of composure before she faced him.

But Matt's attention was on the slim, fair-haired man who had joined him at the bar. As Clea watched she saw the other man grin widely as he lifted his hands and sketched two curved shapes like the sides of a figure eight in the air, the gesture making Matt throw back his head and laugh aloud. Clea's lips tightened, her hand gripping her bag until her knuckles showed white. There was no mistaking the meaning of the gesture, she had seen too many men describe the female form in that way—generally with some lascivious comment accompanying the movement—to be in any doubt. Her head came up proudly and, her decision made without her quite being aware of it, she moved forward purposefully into the bar.

Matt's dark head swung round at the sound of the door opening, his eyes skimming over her swiftly and appraisingly before he pushed back his cuff and looked pointedly at his watch. Irritation sparked fire in Clea's green eyes.

'I'm sorry if I'm a little late,' she said stiffly, her tone implying that she was no such thing. 'Have you been waiting long?'

'A while,' was the smoothly drawled answer. 'But I can assure you you're well worth waiting for.'

I'd expected something rather more original from you, Mr Highland, Clea thought to herself. And flattery will get you nowhere—particularly not when it was accompanied by another of those boldly assessing surveys of her body in the elegant white suit and scarlet blouse. As on that first meeting nine years before, Matt had risen to his feet at her entry, but Clea was no longer a naïve little schoolgirl who took such meaningless actions as a sign of a perfect gentleman. It took more than surface gestures of courtesy to make a man she could respect.

'Would you like a drink?' Matt was every inch the urbane host, totally at ease, while she was as prickly as a hedgehog, those derogatory words spoken nine years before still sounding in her mind as clearly as if it had been only yesterday. Looking at him now, so dark and sleek in his expensive suit, she wondered if he ever recalled the young girl he had met so briefly and if he had ever asked himself why she had never come down the next morning but had stayed in her room, complaining of feeling unwell. She hadn't been able to face him again, she recalled, and the memory made her want to snap that no, she didn't want a drink, she didn't want anything from him.

But she had to be polite—even friendly—to him for a while at least if she was ever going to carry out her plan, and besides, she was thirsty, it had been hot under the lights rigged up for the fashion show. She made herself smile in response to his question.

'Perrier water, please,' she said, and saw his eyebrows lift slightly at her request.

'Nothing stronger?' he questioned, and Clea shook her head firmly.

'No, thanks. Alcohol does nothing for my complexion—or my figure.'

Deliberately she smoothed her hands over her slim hips in the close-fitting pencil skirt, and her mouth twisted cynically as she saw Matt's eyes flick downwards to watch the movement. Men were so obvious, so predictable—and to think that she had once considered this particular man the embodiment of her dreams! Unbidden and unwanted, the memory of that too-tight denim skirt, gaping at the buttons, slid into her mind and she flinched mentally. She didn't want to remember how she had been—but she could never forget Matt's cruel words, and her eyes hardened to emerald chips of ice as he gave her order to the barman, then turned back to Clea, indicating the fair-haired man with a wave of his hand.

'This is my brother-in-law, Chris Lawton. Chris, meet Clea Mallory.'

Clea had held out her hand, a polite smile forming on her lips, when the significance of what Matt had said sank in and froze the smile half-way. His brother-in-law—this man was married to Matt's sister! As she remembered the revealing gesture she had seen Chris Lawton make, it was all she could do to acknowledge his cheerful grin with a cool nod.

'I hoped I'd get to meet you, Miss Mallory. I saw the fashion show—it was quite something!'

'Did your wife enjoy it too?' Clea's tone was cool.

'Liz? No, she couldn't come tonight. She's not very well.'

'Oh, that's a pity.' It was an effort to make the words sound polite. Clea felt a strong pang of sympathy for the absent Liz. How would she have felt if she had seen her husband so obviously describing some voluptuous female in that way?

'Your drink.' Matt's voice sounded in her ear.

'Oh, thanks——' Clea took the glass and sipped the cool, tangy water gratefully, her head buzzing with angry thoughts as she recalled Matt's laughter in response to Chris's gesture. What sort of man was he, to find it amusing when it was made by the man who was married to his own sister?

'Well, I'd better be off.' Chris Lawton drained the last of his drink. 'Liz will be wondering where I've got to, and I'm sure you two want to be alone. It was a pleasure to meet you, Clea. Perhaps Matt will bring you round for dinner some time. I'm sure Liz would be delighted to see you. She was so disappointed to have to miss tonight.'

'I'd like to meet her.'

The words were just a polite gesture, irritation at his assumption that she and Matt would want to be alone prickled in her veins like pins and needles. Suddenly she felt an absurd desire to try to detain Chris, hold him in conversation, anything other than to be left by herself with Matt. But already the other man had turned and with a casual wave was heading for the door.

Clea sipped at her drink again, feeling its sparkling coolness soothe the sudden dryness of her throat. Every nerve seemed alive to the presence of the man at her side, standing so close that her arm brushed his each time she lifted her glass to her lips. She was so accustomed to being as tall as if not taller than almost every man she met that she found his lean height intensely disturbing. He seemed to tower over her, making her feel small and vulnerable, not at all a sensation she was used to.

'Shall we go on up, then?' Matt's quiet words broke in on her thoughts, startling her so that she almost choked on her drink.

'Up?' she questioned sharply, and he nodded.

'I'm staying in the hotel this week to save me having to travel backwards and forwards all the time. I have a suite upstairs, I thought we'd have dinner there.'

Clea swallowed hard, not knowing what to say. When she had accepted Matt's invitation to dinner she had imagined he would take her to some restaurant, a public, impersonal place. To be alone with him in the intimacy of his hotel suite was not at all what she had planned. It implied——

It implied what? Clea caught herself up hastily. That she was more attracted to him than was actually the case? But wasn't that what she wanted, after all? She wanted Matt to think she was attracted to him, wanted him to be attracted to her, and then she was going to drop him flat on his face just as he had done to her all those years ago.

Carefully she conjured up a bright, warm smile, directing it straight into Matt's face, and had the satisfaction of seeing his grey eyes darken perceptibly in response.

'I'm ready,' she said lightly.

Matt's hand rested on the back of her waist as he led her out of the bar and towards the lift, she could feel the warmth of his palm through the fine linen of her suit and had to fight against the impulse to twist away from that possessive touch. Instead she did exactly the opposite, leaning back slightly so that the light pressure was increased, and she felt Matt's fingers move slightly in a caressing motion against the small of her back.

'What did you think of the show?' she asked as the lift glided upwards—not to the first floor this time, she noticed as Matt pressed the button marked with the number six.

'I thought it went very well.' His tone was noncommittal and for a second Clea felt a stab of pique. She had expected more than that from him.

'Did you like the red dress?' she continued, trying to lead him on, picturing the scarlet silk sheath with its low

V-neckline and daringly slit skirt in her mind. The dress had exposed a great deal of pale, satiny flesh and it was just the sort of dress that would appeal to any man she believed.

A smile flickered across Matt's hard face. 'I much preferred the blue one,' he murmured drily, a gleam of humour in his dark eyes that told Clea that he had been well aware of the direction of her thoughts.

'But that covered me from head to toe!' she exclaimed in surprise.

'Exactly.' Matt's eyes met hers directly, that glint of amusement intensifying disturbingly. I find that subtle suggestion is far more sexy than any blatant display. When a woman is as beautiful as you are she doesn't have to put all her attraction out in the open like goods in a shop window.' The dark eyes slid downwards deliberately, moving slowly over her body. 'A man prefers to think that such delights are kept for his eyes only.'

For a second Clea was incapable of any response. She had been angling for a compliment and he had known it and given her one—but the way he had done it had turned it back on itself, so that instead of being flattered she felt as if she had experienced a deliberate put-down.

'The red dress is the high spot of the show,' she declared almost defensively. 'Everyone considers it Raphael's best design this year.'

'Perhaps it is,' drawled Matt as the lift came to a halt. 'But I definitely preferred the blue one.'

He had surprised her, Clea admitted to herself as she followed him down the corridor. She had genuinely believed that no man could have resisted the red dress, and Matt's choice of the long-sleeved, high-necked blue one had frankly amazed her. How many other surprises might he have in store for her? That was a speculation that did little to ease the fluttering sensation in her stomach as she stepped through the doorway and into the suite beyond.

The room she had seen on the previous night had been attractive enough, but this one, on the top floor of the hotel, was magnificent. It was decorated in the same tones as room seventeen, but it comprised a suite of three rooms, the lounge in which she stood, a double bedroom and a luxuriously appointed bathroom. A huge window filled almost all of the opposite wall and through it Clea could see the lights of London spread out below her.

'Make yourself comfortable.' Matt had removed his jacket, slinging it carelessly over the back of the nearest chair, and he tugged his tie loose at his throat as he crossed the room to pick up a burgundy leather-bound menu that was lying on a coffee table.

'Have a look at this and see what you'd like to order,' he said, holding it out to her.

Clea barely spared the menu a glance. Her composure, already threatened by Chris Lawton's revealing gesture, had been further rocked by Matt's comment about the red dress, and she wasn't sure she could eat anything.

'Just chicken salad will be fine.'

A frown creased Matt's forehead. 'Are you sure that's all you want? You're painfully thin.'

'I am *slim*, not thin.' Clea's tone was tart. 'I need to be for my job.' Green eyes met grey, hers sparkling with defiance, Matt's soberly thoughtful. 'Just chicken and salad, please,' she repeated firmly.

'Dinner won't be long,' Matt said a short time later after ordering their meal through room service. 'Would you like a drink while we wait?'

Clea considered carefully. She wanted to charm this man, win him over, but if she was to do that she would have to relax. The tightness of the muscles at the back of her neck warned her just how tense she was. Perhaps a glass of wine would help.

'Some white wine would be lovely.'

'So tell me about yourself,' said Matt when their drinks had been poured and he was seated in the chair opposite her. 'Have you any family?'

Clea took a sip of her wine as a delaying tactic, thinking rapidly. She had known this would come, so how was she going to handle it? It was probably best—and safest—to stay as close to the truth as possible.

'My parents and one brother. They don't live in London, though, they're—up north.'

At least her mother and Ned were, she added privately to herself, but she couldn't risk admitting that Barry was now living and working in America, because Matt might know that. She wasn't sure whether he and Barry were still in contact with each other. After that fateful visit she had never mentioned Matt to her stepbrother again, and when Barry had offered her a trip to London as her eighteenth birthday present she had carefully found reasons to avoid going. Very soon after that he had taken the American job. Her parents had heard from Matt a couple of times after his visit and he had sent a card most Christmases, but since Barry had moved all direct contact had been broken off.

'Did you always want to be a model?' Matt was asking.

'Oh, no—when I was at school I had no idea what I wanted to do, and besides I——' Clea broke off abruptly taking another hasty sip of her wine to cover her near mistake. She had been about to say, 'I was too fat and ugly to think of being a model,' but that would have given too much away.

'You?' Matt prompted as she hesitated.

'I—didn't think I had a chance. It's a fiercely competitive

world.'

'So how did you end up in it?'

'I won a competition organised by a magazine. I really only entered it for a laugh—it was my mother's idea—but to my astonishment I got first prize, a modelling assignment with the magazine—and——' she spread her hands wide '—the rest is history.'

But history carefully tailored to suit the occasion, she thought to herself, thankful for the fact that a knock at the door announcing the arrival of their meal distracted Matt's attention from her for a few much-needed minutes of peace and quiet in which to push a few facts firmly to the back of her mind.

She had said nothing of the year before the competition, a year spent in strict dieting and rigorous exercise. She had joined an aerobics class, read every article on beauty care she could lay her hands on and had applied the lessons she had learned with an almost religious fervour, acquiring a great deal of self-discipline along the way.

Her mother, surprised at first by this sudden complete turnaround from her former lackadaisical ways, had encouraged and supported her, paying for regular trips to the best local hairdresser they could find. Graham had been the first to cut her hair in the sleek, smooth bob that was easily adaptable to so many styles, giving her that slightly Egyptian look which the competition judges had picked up and which had made Clea decide to revert to her proper name for her modelling work.

It was lucky she had, Clea reflected; she could never have pulled off this decption otherwise. She shifted uneasily in her seat, her stomach churning at the thought of the possible repercussions if Matt did recognise her. But really, she consoled herself, she had nothing to fear. Matt's behaviour was not that of a man who had the slightest suspicion who she was.

On the contrary, he appeared to be every bit as attracted to her as she could wish. Clea allowed herself a small, secret smile of triumph at the way things were going.

She kept the conversation light during the meal, sticking strictly to stories of her years in London and so avoiding the traps that lay in any account of her childhood and home life. It was easily done, she had a fund of tales of her travels, the sometimes exotic locations in which she had posed for photographs, and she spiced her conversation with drily witty accounts of the problems of modelling clothes in the wrong seasons, shivering in a swimsuit on a bitterly cold day or sweltering in furs in the middle of a heatwave. Her story of one particular disaster had Matt throwing back his head and laughing aloud.

'That must have made a wonderful photograph!' he said when she had recounted how she had posed at the end of a pier and the railing against which she had leaned had given way, toppling her backwards into the sea just as the camera clicked.

'It did.' It was a struggle to keep her voice light. When he smiled like that she could almost forget what he was really like, the gleam of amusement that lightened those dark eyes having a strange effect on her breathing, making it rapid and uneven. 'When the prints came out all you could see was a pair of feet in the most ridiculously expensive shoes. They were ruined, of course—and so was my make-up.'

Her face sobered, another unwanted memory surfacing in her mind. She had looked a wreck when they had fished her out of the sea, her make-up streaked all over her face, her hair hanging in limp rats' tails, and as she had made her way back up the beach, water dripping from her clothes and her shoes making a dreadful squelching sound, she had come face to face with Simon. She would never forget the look of disconcerted horror that had crossed his face. Simon was a man who liked beautiful things, his house was full of the antiques he had collected over the years and, Clea admitted painfully to herself, she had been just another item to add to that collection. It had been that evening that he had told her their relationship was over.

The memory left a sour taste in her mouth, and abruptly she pushed her plate away from her, her appetite deserting her even though her meal was only half finished.

'Is that all you're going to eat?' Matt frowned his disapproval, his eyes going to her discarded plate.

'I've had as much as I want.' Defiance rang in Clea's voice. 'I've never had much of an appetite.'

That wasn't strictly true. In the early days of her diet it had been a terrible struggle to go without the sort of food she enjoyed. She had dreamed of savoury pizzas or a large helping of spaghetti bolognese. But it hadn't been any thought of calorie-counting that had made her lose her appetite now.

'Women don't need as many calories as men,' she added when Matt's frown did not lighten. She was well aware of the substantial meal he had eaten, evidently enjoying his food, and yet his lean body hadn't an ounce of excess weight on it.

For a moment it looked as if he was going to continue the argument, but then a shrug dismissed whatever he had been about to say.

'Coffee, then,' he said mildly enough, but there was something lingering deep in the darkness of his eyes that made Clea's nerves tingle as if a cold wind had brushed against them. Perversely she found she was irritated by the way he had dropped the subject. That shrug implied a total indifference that piqued her sharply. She didn't want him to feel indifferent to her!

'Yes, please—black, no sugar,' she told him pointedly, and saw his mouth twist slightly.

'Of course,' he murmured satirically. 'What else?'

They moved from the table to relax as they drank their coffee, and after a moment's hesitation Clea chose to sit on the settee. For now at least she had to pretend that she was attracted to Matt, that she wanted him close to her, and she allowed herself another private smile of triumph when he lowered his long body into the space at her side.

'Do you often take a room in one of your own hotels?' asked Clea, leaning back in her seat and turning to him, letting her eyes meet his directly, using body language to convey the message she wanted him to believe.

'When I'm needed. It's more convenient than commuting from home every day. After this week I'll go back to the house.'

'You don't live in London, then?' This was new. When Barry had talked of Matt he had said that his friend had a flat in London. But then nine years was a long time; it would be unusual if nothing had changed.

Matt shook his dark head. 'I've had enough of the city to last me a lifetime. I like to escape to the country when I can. Don't you find you miss it?'

'Miss it?' Clea echoed faintly, her mind working overtime on the suspicion that he knew after all; that he remembered Patti and her home in a small northern village. Her mouth was suddenly dry and she had to swallow hard to relieve the uncomfortable sensation. Matt's closeness and the subject of their conversation were reviving unwelcome memories of their very first meeting when they had talked on just this topic. A wave of embarrassment filled her as she recalled her own gauche attempts to appear sophisticated, her declaration that she found living in the country boring.

'There are plenty of cities in the north,' she said coolly. 'Some of them every bit as sophisticated as London. Why do southerners always think civilisation ceases north of Watford?'

'That wasn't what I said.' Matt's tone made the words a mild reproof. 'And I'm not completely ignorant of the attractions of the north. I had a very good friend whose family lived in Yorkshire, and I own a cottage in the Dales myself.'

'Do you?' The words came out rather breathlessly, Matt's mention of a very good friend coming a little too close to the bone for comfort. Clea hoped that her defence of northern cities had led him to believe that she had lived in one of them. She didn't want him to start thinking of Barry and his visit to their home because he might remember Barry's sister. 'I don't suppose you find the time to get up there very often?'

Relief flooded through her as she saw Matt shake his head. Yorkshire was a large county, but all the same she was having difficulty adjusting to the idea that he might have been up north, possibly even fairly close to where she lived, and she had never known.

But then she had only stayed in the village for a year or so after his visit. Then she had moved to London, and although she tried to get home as often as she could the pressure of work made it impossible to manage it with any real frequency. Clea was suddenly overwhelmed by an unexpected feeling of homesickness that stung so sharply that tears pricked at her eyes.

'Not as often as I'd like,' she heard Matt saying as if through a cloud of cotton wool that seemed to fill her mind. 'I manage to snatch the odd weekend here and there, but it isn't enough. I use the cottage as a retreat—to get away from everything. There's no phone and the nearest village is seven miles away. When I'm there no one can reach me. I can forget about Highland Hotels and just relax.'

'So what do you do with yourself when you're there?' Clea was genuinely intrigued. This was a side of Matt she hadn't expected to discover. Her overriding impression of him was of a high-powered businessman, absorbed in his work, thriving on the bustle and noise of London. She had taken his comments on living in the country at their first meeting as simply polite conversation;

'I read, listen to music, walk for miles, work in the garden—all the things I don't find the time to do here.'

'It sounds—idyllic.'

Clea hadn't meant her comment to sound satirical. Her mental adjustment to this unexpected side of Matt's character had combined with happy memories of doing just the sort of things he described in her happy, more innocent childhood to make the words come out very differently from the way she had planned, and a swift, probing glance from those grey eyes had her wishing she had had more control over her voice.

'It is. Perhaps you'd like to spend a weekend there some time?'

'I'd like that.'

She sounded more enthusiastic this time, a picture of the moors near her home forming in her mind as she spoke. As a teenager she had often gone for long tramps across those moors, revelling in the space and the silence, loving the blend of purple and green in a shadowy mass of colour, enjoying the sense of freedom, the feeling of the wind in her hair. Homesickness stabbed at her once more. It was a long time since she had been so at one with her surroundings.

'Well, perhaps we could arrange something——'

'It won't be easy,' Clea put in hastily, pushing her memories to the back of her mind with an effort. She had no desire to be alone with this man in the isolated cottage he had described. 'As I told you yesterday, I'm very heavily booked up for the next few weeks. I won't have any free time before August at the earliest.'

'Well, there's no rush,' Matt responded easily. 'I've plenty of commitments myself. August would suit me fine. We can sort the details out later.'

Clea murmured something that might have been assent, too disconcerted by this unexpected complication to form any coherent answer. She hadn't planned on committing herself to a holiday with Matt, and yet somehow she seemed to have done just that. Still, she told herself, August was almost two months away. A lot could happen in six weeks. If things went according to plan she wouldn't even be around in Matt's life by then. When a pang of disappointment at the thought of missing a trip to the Dales twisted her heart she squashed it down hastily. She could always visit her mother and Ned if she was so desperate to see Yorkshire again.

Something soft brushing her cheek jolted her out of her thoughts with a start, her discomposure increased by the realisation that what she had felt had been the touch of Matt's hand, his fingers trailing lightly down her face from temple to jaw, lingering under her chin and turning her face towards him.

He's going to kiss me, she thought, her mind suddenly cool and detached. She had known this moment would come—in fact, by her position on the settee, her voice, her movements, she had actively encouraged it—but that didn't prevent her stomach from clenching nervously at the memory of that other, determined assault on her lips.

Relax! Her mind transmitted the message to her body just in time to prevent the instinctive tensing of her muscles as Matt slid closer, his free arm coming round her shoulders to draw her nearer to him. She had to look as if she was enjoying this, as if it was what she had wanted all evening. Deliberately she tilted her head, offering her mouth and he was not slow to take her up on her silent invitation.

His lips were warm and firm as they closed over hers, softly at first, but then with an increasing pressure that opened her mouth under his, allowing the intimate invasion of his tongue at the same moment as his strong fingers tangled in her hair, twisting in the blue-black silken strands as he pressed her close up against the firm wall of his chest. He was very good at this, that strangely uninvolved part of Clea's mind registered; he had obviously had a great deal of practice. But if she was to make him believe that the attraction he felt for her was mutual she should make some move, not just sit here like a block of wood.

It was surprisingly easy to lift her arms and entwine them round his neck, to let her fingers stroke the soft dark hair at the nape of his neck, and she felt him smile against her lips as he sensed her touch. Immediately a flame of anger lit up inside her. He was so sure of himself, so smugly arrogant, so conviced that no woman would be able to resist him. Well, she would show him!

Deliberately she increased the pressure of her mouth on his, tongue meeting tongue in silent provocation as she let herself relax into his hold, her body soft and pliant against his hardness, knowing a glow of triumph at his swift response. But that was her last coherent, detached thought, for as Matt's hands moved to cover her breasts her mind hazed over as if a mist had suddenly filled it and she felt the warmth of his touch like a scorching fire through the thin material of her blouse, burning the delicate flesh beneath it. Unconsciously she sighed, her fingers twisting in his hair, pulling his head down even closer until at last, reluctantly, he had to draw away to catch his breath.

'God, but you're beautiful!'

Matt's voice was thick and husky, his tone uneven, and

at those words, the words of her adolescent dreams, reality flooded back into Clea's thoughts with a suddeness that was sickeningly painful, making her mind reel. With a tiny shake of her head she cleared her mind of the haze of delight that had clouded it and forced herself to think rationally before it was too late. She had planned on this happening, had wanted Matt to react in this way—but she hadn't expected to enjoy it!

Cautiously she looked up into Matt's eyes and saw how they had deepened to black with the desire that burned in him. Immediately an alarm sounded in her head. Things had gone far enough. She had to call a halt before—— Her mind slid away from the contemplation of what might result. She had wanted to encourage Matt, give him enough rope to hang himself, but not all at once. It was better to take things more slowly. She could read Matt's feelings in the darkness of his eyes; there was no mistaking the fire of passion that burned there. As he reached for her again she turned her head in an apparently spontaneous but in fact carefully planned movement to glance at her watch.

'Heavens! Is that the time?'

With a supple movement she neatly avoided his grasp, slipped out of his encircling arms, and got to her feet.

'I have to go.' She aimed for lightness and surprised herself by almost succeeding, only the faintest tremor in her voice betraying anything of the totally unexpected sense of cold loss she felt now that she was away from the warmth of Matt's body. She tried to smile into his eyes, but her composure wavered as she saw them narrow swiftly, the muscles in his jaw tightening ominously. With a determined effort she drew herself up. She had known he would not be pleased—in fact that was the effect she had hoped for. The more frustrated he felt now, the more likely he was to continue the chase—and she would let him pursue her until, just at the moment when he thought he'd caught her, she would turn the tables on him, show him who was really the hunter and who the prey.

'So soon?'

Clea blinked in surprise at the speed with which Matt had himself under control. It implied a strength of character that she would do well to remember in the future. Matt Highland wasn't going to be quite the pushover she had thought.

'I told you—I have to be in bed by midnight.'

'Ah yes, I'd forgotten you turn into a pumpkin after twelve.' The irony in his tone made Clea's careful smile waver slightly. He stretched lazily and got to his feet. 'Very well, Cinderella, I'll drive you home.'

'I'll get my bag.'

As she crossed the room she caught sight of her reflection in a large mirror that hung on the wall, surprising herself with the sight of her flushed cheeks, an unexpected brightness in her eyes. Her hair was tangled where Matt's hard fingers had ruffled it and her lipstick had vanished completely. She looked disturbingly young and unsophisticated—which was not at all how she wanted Matt to see her.

Busy with the necessary repairs to her appearance, she suddenly became aware of the silence that had descended, making her skin prickle with tension, and, looking beyond her own face in the mirror, she saw that Matt was watching her, his dark eyes narrowed, his expression unreadable, but something about the way he stood, an inexplicable tautness in his muscles, made her stomach muscles tighten uncomfortably. *Had* he recognised her, seen through her to discover the seventeen-year-old Patti? Or was it just that he hadn't recovered his composure as swiftly as she had thought? Hastily she glanced down again, fearful that he might read her uncertainty in her eyes. Behind her she heard him move impatiently.

'Are you ready?' he demanded, his tone brusque and harsh. Then as, still unable to meet his eyes, Clea concentrated on applying a second coat of lipstick with a fine brush he exploded, 'You don't need all that stuff! The hotel's deserted and the streets are pitch black.'

'I always try to look my best!' she retorted, finally swinging round to face him. 'I have an image to keep up—it's part of my job.'

She didn't like the way those steely eyes flicked over her, a flash of something that looked uncomfortably like contempt showing in their darkness. Instinctively she drew herself up to her full five foot ten, ready to defy him further if she had to. But Matt simply shrugged and reached for his jacket.

'It's getting late,' he said expressionlessly. 'If we don't get going the clock will strike twelve—and you know what happened to Cinderella then. Are you coming?' he flung over his shoulder as he headed towards the door.

Her thoughts in turmoil, Clea followed him. What had happened to transform the passionate lover of a few minutes earlier into this coldly distant man? Matt was suddenly as prickly as a hedgehog in a way that could not simply be explained by frustrated desire; he had covered that with an amazing speed and smoothness; and his abrupt change of mood left her with serious doubts about the possible success of her plan. *This* Matt seemed unlikely to want to see her again, let alone lay himself open to the sort of rejection she had planned for him, she thought, glancing across at the taut set of his face as they waited for the lift, Matt standing silent and withdrawn, not even acknowledging her presence with so much as a glance.

His silence lasted throughout the journey to Clea's flat, giving her time to think, reconsider her opinion. He was probably still smarting from her rejection of his advances after all, she told herself. His macho pride had been stung, and he wasn't the sort of man to take that easily. But if he did decide not to see her again it was no skin off her nose. She had done what she wanted, had proved that he was very attracted to her, and by doing so she had laid the ghost of that long-ago humiliation, burying the seventeen-year-old Patti once and for all.

She had so completely convinced herself that the chance of a second date was remote to say the least that it came as a shock when, having parked the car outside her flat, Matt turned to her and said, 'I'd like to see you again. I'm afraid I'll be tied up for the next few days, but after that I'm free. What about Thursday?'

Clea's shake of the head was automatic. Thursday nights were the nights she spent with Maggie, when the two of them took the phone off the hook and let their hair down, relaxing in a way that neither she nor Maggie, in her high-powered job in advertising, could do in their working lives.

'I'm afraid Thursday's out.'

She carefully injected a note of regret into her voice, wanting Matt to believe she was as keen to see him again as he was to see her. She was about to add, 'Any other night would be fine,' but caught herself up hastily. She didn't want to appear *too* eager; far better to tantalise him by keeping him at a distance for a while at least. She rummaged in her handbag for her diary, consulting it in the light of the street lamp under which they were parked.

'Friday's booked up too,' she continued, blithely ignoring

the blank section on the page in front of her. 'But Saturday's clear.'

'Saturday, then. We'll go out for the day somewhere. I'll pick you up about ten.'

No 'please,' no 'if that's all right with you'! Clea thought on a wave of irritation. Matt's invitation had the tone of a command, one he expected to be obeyed without question. But then what else had she expected from a man who had hundreds of employees at his hotels ready to jump to do his bidding if he so much as raised his little finger?

'Saturday it is, then,' she agreed, pushing the diary back into her bag with unnecessary force, using the small action to express her annoyance. As Matt nodded confirmation she pushed open the door. 'Goodnight, Matt—and thank you for the dinner.'

'My pleasure.' The answer came smoothly, but somehow the polite conventionality did nothing to soothe her ruffled feelings. It was only when she was standing on the pavement watching the rear lights of the Jaguar disappear down the road that she realised exactly why she was feeling this way.

She had expected that he would kiss her goodnight, had had her own carefully controlled reaction planned right down to the last detail. She would have been responsive but not eager, coolly pleasant, nothing more—but she had been thwarted by the simple fact that Matt had made no move to touch her, in fact his hand had been on the ignition key even before she had unfastened her seatbelt.

Her green eyes puzzled, Clea shook her head slowly. Matt's behaviour didn't fit with the passion she had sensed burning in him earlier. He seemed to have withdrawn in on himself, deliberately putting a distance between them—and yet he had asked to see her again. Clea's steps were slow, her movements abstracted as she walked to the door and inserted her key in the lock. She was glad to see that no light shone in the downstairs flat. If Maggie was awake and, hearing the door open, came out into the hall to ask how the evening had gone, she had to admit that she would be at a loss as to how to reply.

CHAPTER FIVE

'I SAID wear something casual.' Matt didn't bother with polite greetings when Clea opened the living-room door to him on Saturday morning, and she stiffened at the criticism implicit in his voice.

'This *is* casual,' she retorted sharply, her hands moving instinctively to indicate the white cotton trouser-suit and delicate camisole top she was wearing. When Matt had rung her during the week to say he planned on taking her out into the country for a picnic if the weather was fine she had considered her wardrobe carefully, looking for just the right thing to wear, and had decided that the suit was perfect. But Matt's opinion was quite different, to judge by the look on his face, an expresssion that changed to one of scorn as his gaze came to rest on the delicate white leather sandals on her feet.

'Can you walk in those things?' he demanded, his tone making sparks flash in Clea's green eyes.

'Of course I can! They're beautifully comfortable.'

Behind her back she crossed her fingers against the white lie. The sandals were little more than a few thin strips of white leather and she doubted if she could walk any great distance on the spindly heels. They had cost a near fortune too, but she had fallen in love with them at first sight and had been longing for an opportunity to wear them—and they went perfectly with her outfit.

The dismissive shrug that lifted Matt's wide shoulders drew her attention to his own appearance which, she now realised was not at all what she had expected. A well worn heavy cotton shirt in blue and grey check clung to the firm muscles of his chest, its collar open at the neck revealing the long, tanned column of his throat and a disturbing amount of dark, slightly curling hair. Equally battered denim jeans hung low on his slim hips and on his feet were a pair of navy training shoes that had seen a great deal of wear and looked, Clea admitted a trifle ruefully, very comfortable indeed.

'Are you ready?' A thread of impatience laced Matt's voice. 'It's a lovely day—too beautiful to waste staying indoors.'

'I'm quite ready.' She struggled to smooth the irritation from her tone but only half succeeded. 'But only just—you were early!'

Matt's careless smile dismissed her accusation with infuriating nonchalance. 'Only by a few minutes. It's as near to ten as makes no difference. You've had plenty of time to prepare yourself.'

With an effort Clea closed her lips against a furious retort as she struggled with the anger that threatened to boil up inside her and spill out like molten lava pouring down the sides of a volcano. Did he really think she would be up at dawn in order to be ready, waiting breathlessly for his arrival as his words implied? The arrogance of the man! She was strongly tempted to find some excuse to keep him waiting a while longer, but it would only be a pretence—one that she strongly suspected Matt would see through straight away.

'Is it very hot outside?' she asked. 'Will I need a hat?'

Matt's dark eyebrows shot upwards in stunned surprise. 'A *hat!*' he echoed in frank disbelief. 'Whatever for?'

'To protect my skin.' Clea's tone was tight. She often

wore a wide-brimmed straw hat in the summer because, in spite of her dark colouring, she didn't tan well and she didn't like to risk the drying and ageing effect of too much sun on her face.

He studied her disconcertingly closely, his eyes skimming over the careful colouring and shading that had occupied her for the last twenty minutes.

'Do you think any of the sun's rays are going to get through that lot to burn your skin?' he demanded, the scathing contempt in his voice stinging like the flick of a whip. 'I don't know why you wear the stuff.'

'I like to look——'

'Your best,' he cut in, giving the words a satirical emphasis. 'I know—you told me. It's just that I can't help wondering what you look like without all that warpaint.'

Pale and ordinary. The answer came unprompted into Clea's mind. And rather too much like a slimmed-down version of the Patti Donovan you met all those years ago. That thought put an added sharpness into her voice when she retorted, 'Every woman uses make-up to enhance her appearance. It *isn't* warpaint, as you call it.' Certainly not hers, she added silently to herself. She prided herself on the skilful subtlety with which she applied her make-up. If he had been talking about the heavy-handed colouring Steph had used on her when she was seventeen then he might have a point.

'Isn't it?'

Matt's expression was unreadable and Clea decided that she would be wiser not to try and interpret it or take him up on his taunting question, turning instead to collect her bag, then, after locking her door set off down the stairs, leaving Matt to follow behind.

This hadn't exactly been an auspicious beginning, she

reflected as she crossed the hall. She was supposed to be convincing him that she was attracted to him; instead she had snapped at him like a bad-tempered terrier—hardly the sort of impression she wanted to give him. But it wasn't all her fault, she added indignantly. Matt had to take some of the blame. His comments had been deliberately provocative, calculated to strike sparks off any self-respecting woman. Still, she'd better watch her tongue if she was to have any chance of suceeding in her scheme of revenge. It was harder than she had anticipated to keep her true feelings from showing—and Matt Highland was not turning out quite as she had expected either.

And neither was this trip, she added some time later. When Matt had suggested a picnic she had imagined the grown-up sort of event that she and Maggie occasionally indulged in, taking chicken legs and salad and perhaps some strawberries out on to the patio at the back of the house and eating them in comfort on the garden loungers Maggie had set out there. But when Matt said a picnic he meant a full-blown, traditional countryside picnic with a large hamper of food laid out near where they sat on a rug beside a small, bubbling stream.

If he had made his intentions clear when he had phoned, she might well have dressed differently, Clea thought, ruefully surveying the grass stains on her formerly immaculate white trousers. They had had to tramp what seemed like miles from where he'd parked the car to get here, and she had only walked a few yards before she had realised just what a mistake the white sandals had been. They dug into her feet unmercifully and struggling over the rutted, uneven track—she couldn't even call it a path—had become increasingly difficult as she wobbled precariously on the preposterously high heels. Matt of course had no such problems, his stride lithe and easy as he covered the ground at a fast pace that Clea found impossible to keep up with, in spite of the fact that he was burdened with the hamper and the rug. She was strongly tempted to kick off her shoes and continue in her bare feet, but the thought of giving Matt the opportunity to say 'I told you so' was worse than her discomfort, and she gritted her teeth and plodded on determinedly.

So it was with a secret sigh of relief that she sank down on to the rug that Matt had spread on the grass and stretched her legs out in front of her. Free from the discomfort her feet had been giving her, she was able to admit that they were in a beautiful spot. The sun was warm on her back, the air filled with birdsong, and the stream made a cheerful, friendly noise as it splashed its way down its rocky bed. When she was younger, Clea would have kicked off her shoes, rolled up the legs of her trousers, and gone paddling, delighting in the cool touch of the water on her skin. But those days were long gone, she reflected, a pang of regret for those carefree times stabbing at her so that she turned her head swiftly, staring in frank amazement at the bewildering array of food Matt was unloading from the hamper. 'You've brought enough to feed an army!'

'What's a picnic without food?' he shot back, and something about his tone, the look in his eyes, gave Clea the uncomfortable suspicion that he was testing her in some way.

Did he want to see how strong her resolution was? she wondered as he added a selection of mouthwatering cakes to the array of food he had already laid out. Or had he seen something that remainded him of Patti Donovan so that he was trying to trick her into revealing herself? At seventeen she would have had no hesitation in sampling every one of the delicacies Matt had provided, and Clea's determination to prove herself a very different person combined with the hard-won restraint she had acquired over the years to ensure that she helped herself sparingly to cold meat and salad, painfully conscious of the way Matt was watching her, his steady gaze affecting her composure so that her hand shook slightly as she spooned tomato segments on to her plate.

Remembering his reaction to the dinner she had ordered on the night of the fashion show, Clea found herself tensing, waiting for some critical comment and ready to fling back a sharp retort if he did. But Matt surprised her by keeping silent, though his lips tightened perceptibly when he glanced at her plate. Irritation pricked at her. Why should she care what he thought? she asked herself, annoyed with herself as much as with Matt. The way she ate was her own business and no one else's—except perhaps her agent's.

Her tension eased as, his disapproval apparently forgotten, Matt initiated a light and easy conversation ranging over the events of the past week—a particularly busy week for Clea with an endless stream of photo-sessions so that she had had to dash from one appointment to another with barely time to breathe in between. So now she was glad just to sit and relax, finding it surprisingly easy in Matt's company, his own description of his week lively and interesting, often spiced with a dry wit that had her smiling unreservedly, the smile progressing to spontaneous laughter on several occasions.

So when Matt finally put down his plate and murmured, 'Come here,' his voice softly persuasive, Clea found it seemed the most natural thing in the world to move to his side and rest her head against his shoulder, his arm coming round her waist, warm and strong and unexpectedly enjoyable. She even found herself returning the kisses he drifted across her mouth with an ease that would have seemed impossible only a short time before.

When Matt was like this, she reflected, it was difficult to remember exactly why she was here. He could charm the birds out of the trees with that smile, and his trick of looking straight into her eyes when he spoke made her feel as if she was someone special, someone very important to him.

But a trick was all it was, she reminded herself hastily. She had seen enough reports in the gossip columns over the years to know that Matt Highland was rarely without some female companion, usually some aristocratic beauty or an up-and-coming film star. He probably used his charm on them just as effectively—but not one of them had lasted. In a month or two they had vanished, replaced by some other, equally decorative female. Well, that wasn't going to happen to her. She fully intended that this time the positions would be well and truly reversed.

It was perhaps an hour or so later that Matt glanced up at the sky and frowned.

'I'm afraid the weather's going to let us down. Those clouds look distinctly ominous.'

Startled, Clea followed the direction of his gaze and for the first time she noticed the grey clouds that had gathered, blocking out the sun. Only then did she become aware of the way the warmth had disappeared from the afternoon, a distinct chill pervading the atmosphere so that as Matt moved away from her she felt the loss of the warmth of his body with an intensity that had her shivering in her thin jacket.

'We'd better pack up and get back to the car. It could pour down any minute.'

He was replacing the food containers in the hamper as he spoke, his movements swift and precise. Clea hastened to help him, casting an anxious glance at the sky as she did so. The clouds were thickening by the minute and her mood altered to match the change in the weather, her pleasure in the day driven away by a growing tension that was intensified by the way her hands constantly brushed against Matt's as they repacked the hamper. The frequent brief seconds of contact sent tiny shivers of awareness running down her spine, making her feel colder than ever and twisting her stomach muscles into taut, uncomfortable knots.

She didn't like the way she was feeling, it reminded her too much of the nervous excitement that had gripped her during that first, long-ago meeting with this man, somehow stripping away the intervening nine years and reducing her once more to that gauche and naïve adolescent faced with her fantasy become reality, so that eventually she gave up helping Matt altogether and turned her attention to the rug, shaking it out with brusque, almost aggressive movements before folding it carefully into four.

'Right, that's it.' Matt slung the rug over his shoulder and picked up the hamper. 'Come on, I think we're going to have to run for it!'

The first drops of rain began to fall as they headed back towards the car, Clea stumbling awkwardly in her high-heeled sandals as she struggled to keep up with Matt's long, easy stride. In a vain attempt to protect herself from the rain she held her handbag above her head, but to no avail. In a few minutes her carefully styled hair was hanging limply round her face and cold moisture sprayed her relentlessly, driving into her eyes so that she had to blink hard to clear her vision.

The journey to the car seemed endless, but at last they were there, and Clea scrambled into the front passenger seat, slamming the door with a sigh of relief as Matt bundled the hamper and rug into the boot before sliding into his own seat with a laugh.

'Well, that was a bit sudden!' He shook his dark head, sending tiny drops of rainwater scattering about the car as he moved to start the engine so that the heating could warm them. 'Typical British weather! Not to worry, we'll soon dry out in here, but we'd better let it slacken off a bit before we move.'

Clea barely heard his words. She was hunting through her handbag, looking for her mirror.

'Where would you like to go now?' Matt asked as her hand closed over it and she pulled it out, flipping open its case.

'I don't know . . . ' Her voice trailed away as she saw her reflection. Her wet hair hung like rats' tails and her mascara had run, leaving ugly black smudges round her eyes. Hastily she reached into her bag again, looking for tissues to wipe away the mess.

'Clea?' A note of impatience had slipped into Matt's voice.

'I——'

Ruefully she surveyed her face. The black stains had gone, but so had the rest of her careful make-up, taking with it her self-confidence in a way that made a mockery of her assumption that Patti Donovan was gone for ever. She could never atttract Matt looking like this. 'I want to go home.'

Matt's silence was ominous, threatening, and when she turned to look at him her heart sank as she saw the black frown that darkened his face, his eyes suddenly cold and hard as tempered steel.

'I want to go home,' she repeated, less certainly this time.

'What the hell for?'

'I——My hair's soaking wet——'

'The heating's on, it'll soon dry.' Matt dismissed her explanation curtly.

Yes, it would dry, but not in the sleek style she liked. When left to dry naturally her hair kinked into uncontrollable waves, becoming slightly wild and rather too much like the tangled mane it had been when Matt had first met her.

'I want to go home.' Stubbornness tightened the muscles in her face, making the words come out high and sharp. 'I'm wet and cold and I——'

'Damnation, Clea!' his angry voice cut in on her. 'It was just a rainstorm, nothing to get hysterical about. It's passing already. You won't melt.'

'I'm not hysterical!' she snapped back, feeling raw from the sarcasm in his tone. 'And I know I won't melt—but that doesn't alter the fact that I'm cold and uncomfortable. All I want is to have a hot bath and get into some dry clothes, and the sooner the better, so I would be grateful if you'd just start the damned car and take me home!'

For a long silent moment green eyes locked with grey, Matt's coldly thoughtful, Clea's sparkling with indignation, her mouth set in a mutinous line. Then at last he shrugged and turned away, his hand going to put the car into gear. Clea's temper threatened to get the better of her. She intensely disliked that way he had of shrugging his shoulders so carelessly. It made her feel as if she had been dismissed as not worth bothering about, too much like young Patti Donovan for comfort. This must be how Matt would act when he had decided that a relationship must end, coldly detached, indifferent to anyone else's feelings. But it was not going to be that way with her!

The car had begun to move forward and, casting a swift sidelong glance at Matt, his features harshly etched against the window through which the sun was now beginning to shine weakly, Clea gave herself a small mental shake. It would do her no good to quarrel with him now, so early in the relationship. She had to keep him sweet if she was to have any change of carrying out her plan. But a second, more thoughtful, glance at that unyielding profile, seeing the tightness of the muscles in his jaw that drew his mouth into a thin, hard line, made her wonder if she wanted to go through with this anyway. Matt Highland made her feel uncomfortable, a bewildering confusion of feelings tangling up inside her mind so that she couldn't separate one from another. Perhaps it would be easier simply to forget the idea.

No! She rejected the thought even as it formed in her mind. It might be easier, but it definitely wouldn't be satisfactory. She wanted her revenge for those hateful, hurtful comments he had made, wanted to teach him that he couldn't just treat women as objects without a care for their feelings—but to do that she had to make her peace with him now. With an effort she made herself reach out a hand and gently touch Matt's arm.

'You do understand, don't you?' she said softly. 'You must be soaked through as well.'

Matt's eyes never left the road ahead of him.

'I got a bit wet,' he told her curtly. 'But I'm drying out already.'

That was true. The soft cotton of his shirt was only faintly damp, Clea could feel the warmth of his skin underneath it. The sensation was strangely disturbing, and she was worryingly aware of other things too, the strength of bone and muscle beneath her fingers, the way the damp material clung to the firm lines of his chest and shoulders, the subtle scent of his body so close to hers so that she suddenly felt as if the space in the car had somehow shrunk, becoming confined and restrictive until it was almost claustrophobic. She fought against a need to snatch her hand away as if it had been burned, forcing herself to let it linger caressingly as she murmured, 'It's a pity it's all been spoiled, but there will be other days——'

The swift sidelong glance Matt shot her was unreadable, his face giving nothing away, and Clea felt her heart lurch apprehensively at the thought that perhaps there might *not* be other times, other chances to ensnare him as she wanted to, that her angry words might have ruined all her schemes. Hastily she set herself to repair the damage she had so unthinkingly caused

'It was a lovely picnic, Matt. I really enjoyed it,' she said soothingly—at least that was the effect she hoped her words would have on him.

Matt's stony silence was not encouraging. His muscles tensed as he steered the car around a corner, the movement pulling his arm away from her so that her hand dropped to the seat beside him.

'The food was wonderful,' Clea tried again. 'You must thank your——'

'You barely ate enough of it to judge!' Matt bit out, breaking his silence at last.

Not again! What was this obsession he had with what she ate? Clea swallowed down the sharp protest that rose to her lips.

'But I enjoyed what I did eat. I enjoyed the whole day.'

She surprised herself by finding how little effort she had to make to put the ring of conviction into her voice. She *had* enjoyed herself, she realised with a sense of shock.

'It doesn't have to end yet.'

Matt's attention was still on his driving, but his voice had softened slightly, becoming rather less clipped and curt, and Clea could not suppress the smile of triumph that curved her lips. She was winning him round. For a moment she was tempted to reconsider her decision to go straight home. If she had more time to work on the opening he had given her—— But then she felt her hair, already partly dry in the warmth of the car. It was beginning to curve, to coil into the waves she so disliked.

'I really do need to get warm and change my clothes.'

Did she sound regretful enough? She really wanted Matt to think she was genuinely sorry that their day together had been cut short, that she would have liked to spend more time in his company, but had she succeeded? She couldn't judge; Matt's face was a stiff, withdrawn mask and she had no hope of gauging his reaction.

The rest of the journey was completed in total silence, a silence that preyed on Clea's nerves, twisting them into uncomfortable knots so that when the car finally pulled up outside her flat she found that her fingers had coiled into tight fists, her nails digging into her palms.

'Here you are, home and dry.' She could not be unaware of the deliberate irony of Matt's words. Her jacket and trousers were already almost completely dry and, with the typical perversity of an English summer, the sun was once more shining brightly, warming the afternoon. As she hesitated, uncertain of her next move, the sound of Matt's fingers drumming restlessly on the steering wheel seemed unnaturally loud and somehow threatening.

'Thank you again for a lovely picnic.'

'My pleasure.'

Once again that conventionally polite phrase seemed to hide innumerable things left unsaid. Just what was in Matt's mind? Did he plan to see her again, or had she blown it completely? For a moment she sat there, waiting, for what she wasn't quite sure. Matt made no move to take her in his arms and kiss her goodbye. He appeared abstracted, distant, his thoughts unflatteringly elsewhere, and fighting the urge to round on him, demand to know exactly what was wrong, Clea made herself open the door and get out of the car.

'Goodbye, Matt.'

Tension, uncertainty, and annoyance at the way he made her feel so uncomfortable, so unsure of what to do, made her voice cold and proud. Matt lifted one hand in silent acknowledgement, then before she had time to step back he swung the car away from the kerb and headed off down the road. Clea's mouth tightened to an angry line.

'Damn the man!' she muttered furiously to herself. He hadn't even had the courtesy to say goodbye! So much for her plan of trapping him, turning the tables on him. Well, she had better things to do with her time than to waste it playing games with a man who was so full of his own self-importance that he spared no thought for other people's feelings! She was well rid of him, she told herself, and the strange, empty feeling in the pit of her stomach was simply a reaction to the thwarting of her plan of revenge, nothing more. There could be no other possible reason for it; she certainly wasn't sorry that her relationship with Matt had ended so abruptly—if anything, she was glad to be rid of him!

A long, warm bath did a great deal to restore Clea's

composure. She lingered in the perfumed water, feeling her taut muscles relax, letting the tangle in her mind unravel until she felt refreshed and more at peace with the world. It was a relief to know that Matt Highland was out of her life—for good this time. The strain of keeping up a pretence of liking him had been responsible for the tension she had felt whenever she was with him.

But it hadn't all been a strain. Clea's hands stilled on the soft towel with which she was drying herself as she recalled the ease with which she and Matt had talked during dinner the previous weekend and again today before the rainstorm had so abruptly interrupted things. She had enjoyed those times, responding easily to Matt's intelligent, witty conversation—but that didn't mean that she regretted the fact that it was all over, she told herself, using the towel briskly. He was an accomplished charmer, a perfect host, a pleasant companion, but that sociable façade hid a self-centred, arrogant interior. Her movements became more brusque, rubbing her skin with a force that made it glow. She would have loved the chance to have brought him down a peg or two, letting him see what rejection felt like for the first time in his life.

She was dressed in jeans and a light cotton shirt when the doorbell rang, making her pause in the act of brushing her hair, now carefully restored to its usual smooth, shining cap around her face.

'Who could this be?' She spoke the question aloud, glancing at her reflection in the mirrror with a small, puzzled frown. The face that looked back at her was scrubbed clean of make-up, her cheeks a soft, glowing pink. She looked about fifteen, she thought wryly—then jumped as the bell rang again, sounding harsh and strident in the still afternoon.

'All right, I'm coming!' She addressed the unseen caller as she headed for the door. Clearly Maggie was out, otherwise she'd have opened the door by now.

Clea caught a vague glimpse of a dark-haired figure through the mottled glass of the door before she opened it, but that failed to prepare her for the shock of seeing Matt, tall and broad and totally unexpected, standing on the doorstep.

'Oh!' Clea's heart lurched violently as she took a step backwards, one hand going up to her face, her eyes widening in amazement. She felt stunned, as if she had walked straight into a solid brick wall. 'H-hello.'

The feeling of disorientation increased as she looked into Matt's dark eyes and saw them travel over her face, narrowing swiftly in an echo of her own surprise, then lingering, suddenly strangely intent. If she hadn't known better she might have thought that he had never seen her before, and that thought, when combined with his searching scrutiny, was so unnerving that her heart set up a frantic pounding, making her next words come out on a shaky gasp.

'What—what are you doing here?'

'You left this in the car.' Matt reached into his pocket and pulled out a slim gold wristwatch. 'I thought you might need it, so I brought it back.'

His gaze still hadn't left Clea's face and she felt suddenly and irrationally fearful as if he might be able to probe deep behind her eyes and read her mind. She was also painfully conscious of the fact that she was not looking her best. Her thoughts flew back to the image of herself she had seen in the mirror. Did she look too much like Patti? Would Matt recognise her and ruin her plans once and for all?

'That's always happening.' The words tumbled over each

other as she forced them out, her tongue feeling strangely thick and clumsy. 'I think the clasp must be loose—I'd better get it seen to. Thank you for bringing it round.'

'It was no trouble.' Matt's tone was smoothly polite but, watching him closely, Clea thought she saw a flicker of some inexplicable emotion deep in the darkness of his eyes. It was there and gone again before she could even begin to attempt to interpret it, so that she wondered if it had ever really been there at all or if she had been imagining things. 'I had nothing else to do.'

Nothing *better* to do, Clea amended in the privacy of her own thoughts, a prickle of irritation running through her, the touch of anger clearing her mind of the last shreds of shock at his unexpected appearance so that for the first time she saw him clearly. He really was stunningly attractive, she thought inconsequentially, her mind noting automatically the sensual appeal of a tall, well-built frame, those deep grey eys, and the way the sunlight brought out the shine on the glossy dark hair. He was the sort of man any woman would be proud to be seen with, she admitted, and knew a sudden, intense wish that she had put on something more flattering than her old jeans and had had time to do her face properly. He had caught her very much at a disadvantage, and that was not all how she wanted to feel with this man.

'I——'

'Clea——'

Clea's hesitant beginning and Matt's use of her name coincided exactly, causing them both to break off and stand silently, unsure of how to continue. But before the silence could become uncomfortable a cheery call reached them from further down the street. Maggie was coming towards them, several bulging carrier bags in her hands.

'Hi there!' she smiled brightly as she came up to

them. 'Back already? Did you get rained off?'

Clea frowned slightly as she saw her friend's eyebrows shoot upwards as she took in her lack of make-up and less than elegant attire. She didn't need Maggie's reaction to reinforce the fact that this was not the image she wanted to present to Matt.

'We got caught in the downpour and had to come home.' She kept her eyes fixed on Maggie's face, suddenly afraid to look at Matt, unsure of what she might see in his eyes. 'I left my watch in Matt's car—the catch was loose and it must have slipped from my wrist—so he very kindly brought it back.' She was uncomfortably aware of the way her tongue was running away with her, revealing too much of the disturbed state of her thoughts.

'Well, I'm dying for a coffee. Would you like to join me?' Maggie's invitation clearly included Matt as well, and Clea silently cursed her friend's casual generosity. She didn't think she could cope with much more of Matt's unsettling company today, particularly not the way she was feeling right now. She needed time to pull herself together, make herself look presentable, and then perhaps she could face him with more confidence—if she ever saw him again, she added hastily, remembering his earlier departure without a hint of another invitation. Dimly she became aware of his polite refusal.

'I'm afraid I have to get back. Perhaps some other time.' His words were accompanied by another of those direct, searching looks at Clea's face.

Did he really have to go, or was he too not keen on spending any more time in *her* company than he already had? And did that 'some other time' include Clea as well? Was he hinting that, after all, he would like another date. Clea didn't know what to think, and her uncertainty made her take refuge in a hasty step backwards, letting Maggie in and turning towards the door to her friend's flat as if taking up that invitation to coffee was the only thing on her mind.

'Goodbye, Matt,' she said over her shoulder. 'And thanks again for bringing my watch back—— Here, let me help you with those,' she added as Maggie struggled with her shopping as she hunted for her key.

In the confusion of taking hold of two over-full and awkward bags, Clea didn't see the moment when Matt left, but she heard his car roar off down the street, the sound of its engine like an exclamation of exasperated anger in her ears.

'So that was the infamous Matt Highland!' Maggie collapsed into a chair and kicked off her shoes. 'He's *gorgeous*, kiddo! I nearly fainted away when I opened the door this morning and saw him there. I was strongly tempted to tell him you weren't at home and entice him in here to have him all to myself. He is one amazing hunk of a man!'

'I told you he was good-looking!' Clea's tone was uncharacteristically sharp; the thought of Maggie 'enticing' Matt was strangely unsettling. 'But it's not what a parcel's wrapped in that counts—it's what's inside that's important—and inside Matthew Highland is an arrogant, self-centred creature without a thought for anything beyond himself.'

'If you say so.' Maggie sounded disappointed. 'But I must say it's a terrible pity. So you're still set on the idea of bringing him down, are you?'

I doubt if I'll get the chance, Clea was about to declare, but she hesitated, recalling the look on Matt's face as he spoke her name. Just for a second his expression had softened, becoming almost warm, and there had been an unexpected light in those grey eyes, the recollection of which heated her blood suddenly, sending a wash of colour into her cheeks. What had he been about to say? What *would* he have said if they hadn't been interrupted by Maggie's ill-timed arrival? Had he been about to ask to see her again? And if he had, how would she have answered him?

'I don't know,' she said slowly, as much in response to her own question as to Maggie's. 'To tell you the truth, Maggs, I just don't know.'

CHAPTER SIX

CLEA was in the kitchen, putting the final touches to the meal she and Maggie were to share, when the telephone rang sharply.

'I'll get it,' Maggie called from the living-room, and she heard the receiver being lifted and her friend's voice giving the number.

'Yes, she's here—hang on a sec—Clea!'

Maggie waved the receiver high in the air as Clea appeared in the doorway in answer to her summons.

'It's *him!*' she mouthed silently, her eyebrows shooting upwards, her face a picture of excited glee.

Him. Clea's heart thumped unevenly as she crossed the room to take the receiver from Maggie's grasp. There was only one person her friend would describe in that way, giving such an emphasis to the word. But why should Matt be ringing her now? It was over a week since the day of the picnic and she had heard nothing from him in all that time. She had stopped even wondering if he would call, had tried to put all thought of him out of her mind—though she hadn't fully succeeded on that score, she admitted. She had often found her thoughts straying to that moment at the door, wondering what Matt had been about to say.

'Hello.' Confusion made her voice weak and shaken.

'Clea?' In contrast, Matt's tone was firm and confident as ever. 'Hi—how are you?' Not waiting for an answer to his question, he continued, 'I was wondering if you'll be free on Friday.'

'I'm not sure,' Clea replied, stalling for time in order to collect her scattered thoughts and deliberately ignoring the fact that only minutes before the phone had rung she had been telling Maggie that for once she actually had that whole day clear, no appointments, just the welcome prospect of a free long weekend. 'Why?'

'I've just been talking to Chris—you remember, my brother-in-law. You met him the night of the fashion show.'

'Oh yes, I remember.' Clea's hand tightened on the receiver. She recalled Chris Lawton perfectly, just as she remembered that revealing gesture that had caused Matt so much amusement.

'Then you'll recall that he suggested we all had dinner together so you could meet Liz. He's invited us for Friday night.'

'He's invited us!' Fury suffused Clea's mind at the offhand arrogance of the words. No apology for not having contacted her all week, no 'would you like to come', just an assumption that she would come if she could.

'I don't think——' she began, then caught herself up sharply, her plan of revenge, shelved because of Matt's apparent lack of interest, surfacing in her mind. She *would* go, damn it! She wasn't doing anything that evening and she had to admit that she had been piqued by Matt's silence, feeling frustrated at the way her scheme had been thwarted before it had really had a chance to get off the ground. Now, unknowingly, Matt was offering her a second chance. 'Look, can you hang on while I check my diary?'

Clea put the receiver down on the table and turned to Maggie, who had been listening shamelessly to the part of the conversation she could hear, undisguised curiosity stamped on her face.

'Well?'

'He wants me to have dinner with him and his sister and her husband,' Clea told her, speaking softly for fear that, even at the other end of the telephone wires, Matt might hear.

'Meet the family, eh?' Maggie looked as if she was about to burst into a fit of giggles. 'Strikes me Mr Highland is getting serious. So—are you going?'

'I'm not sure.' Clea frowned thoughtfully. *Was* Matt 'getting serious', as Maggie had put it! Certainly that 'us' had implied that they were a couple, in his mind at least, and an invitation to meet his family could be interpreted as an indication of the fact that he was rather more than indifferent as she had assumed. And if he was then it was all the better for Clea—she wouldn't have to wait too long before putting her plan into action. 'Shall I?'

Maggie's grin was wide and conspiratorial. 'Go on!' she urged.

Clea found herself smiling in response. Decisively she picked up the phone again.

'Matt? I find I'm free on Friday——'

Elizabeth Lawton was not at all what she had imagined when she had tried to picture Matt's sister, Clea reflected as she studied her hostess across the highly polished dinner table. Liz had none of her brother's imposing height or his dark colouring; instead she was at least four inches shorter than Clea herself and her hair and eyes were several shades lighter than Matt's. In fact Clea and Barry looked much more like brother and sister than these two. Knowing Matt, she had expected someone very well groomed and sophisticated, but Liz wore no make-up and her soft brown hair hung in a long, unstyled mane half-way down her back, making Clea think of the old-fashioned pictures of

Alice in Wonderland in a book she had read as a child.

That hair was too heavy, she decided; it swamped Liz's face and detracted from her natural prettiness—and she *was* a pretty woman, or could be with a different hairstyle and the careful use of cosmetics to enhance her eyes and cheekbones. But she didn't know how to make the best of herself. Perhaps that was why her husband had been talking about some other woman. Clea's mouth twisted as she remembered the revealing gesture she had seen Chris make. With a little effort Liz could turn herself into the sort of woman who would keep any man's eyes from straying. After all, she had a very good figure, even if her bust and hips were fuller than was currently fashionable.

'Clea?' Matt's voice broke in on her thoughts, making her start in surprise. Recovering swiftly, she turned an apologetic smile on him

'I'm sorry, I was miles away. What did you say?'

Matt's eyes were deep, impenetrable pools in his shadowed face. The candlelight emphasised his strong bone structure, bringing into stark relief the lines of his cheeks and jaw, making them harder than ever—almost frighteningly so, Clea thought with a shiver of reaction. He had clearly noted her abstracted mood and was none too pleased by it, if the frown that creased the space between his dark brows was anything to go by.

'Liz was saying that everyone thinks modelling's a glamorous job.' Matt's tone was sharp with a hint of reproof. 'But from what you've told me it seems quite the opposite.'

'Oh, yes.' Clea turned to address her remarks directly to her hostess. 'Everyone sees the photographs in magazines and thinks it's just a question of putting on a dress and standing in front of a camera. They've no idea of the work that goes into getting things perfect—it can be terribly wearing trying to look ecstatically happy when your head aches and your feet are killing you. Your smile does tend to become a bit fixed after a few hours.'

'I can imagine.'

Liz's own smile was sweet and gentle. How could Chris think of anyone else! Clea thought angrily, her eyes going to where Liz's husband sat at the far end of the table. Sleek and elegant in a dark blue suit and crisp blue and white striped shirt, Chris Lawton was very much Matt's type, and Clea wondered if that was why Liz had married him. She clearly idolised her elder brother—there was ten years' difference between their ages, Clea had learned during the evening—her rather pale face had lit up with delight when he had entered the room and she hung on every word he said with a flattering attention.

And it was obvious that Matt was very fond of his sister too, Clea admitted, unwillingly notching up a point in his favour. He treated her with a gentle affection that made him appear very different from the dynamic, forceful character she knew. But she couldn't help wondering just how Liz's adoration of her brother would change if she knew about Matt's laughter when Chris had made that crude gesture.

'Shall we have our coffee in the lounge?' Liz was saying. 'If you've all finished, that is. Clea, are you sure you've had enough to eat? You——'

'I've had plenty, thanks,' Clea put in hastily, wanting to forestall the comment on how little she had eaten that was clearly forming on Liz's lips. She could feel Matt's dark eyes on her, the knowledge making her face burn as she continued hurrriedly, 'And it was absolutely delicious. You're a wonderful cook.'

Liz coloured prettily at the compliment.

'I like to cook,' she admitted softly. 'And it's just as well I do. Chris eats like a horse, and as for my big brother, well——' She cast a gently teasing glance at Matt as he stood at her side, towering over her, dwarfing her small figure. 'I doubt if anyone could ever fill him up. But he burns it all off again rushing around all over the place, as I expect you do, Clea.'

'I exercise as well.' Clea found it strangely difficult to keep her voice neutral. For some reason Liz's words and the thoughts of Matt's firm, lithe body they aroused were having a disturbing effect on her equanimity. Her mind would keep straying to picture him as he lounged beside her on the rug on the day of the picnic with the sun shining on his glossy dark hair, warming his skin, and somehow softening the harsh lines of his face.

'Do you go jogging like Matt?' Chris put in. 'He runs miles every day without fail.'

Clea's eyes swung to Matt. So that was how he kept so fit. Unwillingly she acknowledged the way his superbly cut suit hugged the muscular contours of his body, the dark grey material curving round slim hips and long, powerful thighs, then, furious with herself, she dragged her attention back to Chris's question.

'No, I stick to aerobics to keep me fit. I go to a class twice a week and work out at home the rest of the time.'

She had never been keen on jogging. In those early days when she had been so much overweight she had been intensely embarrassed at the thought of slogging round the streets where everyone could see her, and even now she preferred to exercise in the privacy of her own home, not liking to be seen sweating and dishevelled with no make-up and tangled hair. But Matt would look good in a tracksuit, she admitted. There were few people who could wear the loose clothing with success, but his lean frame would be flattered by it.

'I sometimes think I should go to exercise classes,' said Liz. 'But——'

'Everyone should exercise,' Clea put in firmly. 'We only have one body, we owe it to ourselves to keep it in the best possible shape.'

In the tiny silence that followed her words she caught the swift glance that passed between Matt and Chris before Matt moved to put an arm around his sister's shoulders and give her a quick hug.

'You're fine just the way you are, Liz.' Something in Matt's voice drew Clea's eyes to his face and she was disturbed to see the glitter of cold anger deep in their steely darkness as he met her glance before he turned to look down at his sister, a smile warming his face. 'We love you for what you are.'

We love you! Clea clamped down hard on the cynical laugh that threatened to escape her and she viewed that affectionate smile with distinct scepticism. If he was so fond of Liz, how could Matt have laughed when his brother-in-law had described someone else with such obviously lascivious appreciation? Deep inside her resolve to teach Matt a lesson firmed to an icy hardness. Just you wait, Matt Highland, she told him silently. Just you wait!

'I'm sorry, Liz, but it's time to go,' Matt announced some time later, far too soon for Clea, who had been enjoying her conversation with Liz, relaxing in the genuine warmth of the other girl's easy friendliness.

'So soon?' It was Liz who spoke, forestalling Clea's own protest by seconds. 'It's not even half-past eleven!'

'Clea has to get her beauty sleep.' Her brother's tone

was adamant. 'She has a busy day tomorrow.'

She'd been caught in her own trap, Clea admitted to herself, belatedly remembering the imaginary photo-session she had invented during the drive to the Lawtons' home. She had been determined to keep Matt dangling, play hard to get so that he didn't lose interest too soon, which he might do if he thought she was available whenever he wanted. But now her ploy had rebounded. Matt had used it to checkmate her, and she could only nod a silent agreement as she got to her feet.

'I've enjoyed this evening,' said Liz as Chris went to fetch Clea's jacket. 'You must get Matt to bring you again very soon.'

'I'd like that.' The words tasted sour on Clea's tongue. She had taken to Liz from the start, but how was the other girl to feel when she carried out the rest of her plan? Being so obviously devoted to her brother, she wasn't likely to feel too kindly disposed towards someone who treated him as Clea intended to do. It was a great pity; Matt's sister was the sort of woman she would like to have as a friend.

'Perhaps you'd like to come round to my flat for coffee some time when you're in town.' The invitation slipped out before Clea had time to consider whether it was wise or not. 'Just give me a ring to make sure I'm in. I'd be happy to see you any time.'

And perhaps she could do something to help Liz, she reflected privately. A few words of advice, some hints about make-up and hairstyles might prevent Chris's eyes from wandering any further.

'Did you have to drag me away so early?' Clea demanded when they were in the car speeding through the darkened streets, her uncomfortable conscience where Liz was concerned making her voice high and tight.

'You were the one who said you had to be in bed by midnight, Cinderella,' was the smooth reply, effectively rendering her silent, making her feel as if the ground had suddenly crumbled beneath her feet.

She had forgotten that remark, made only as an excuse to get away from Matt, but clearly he recalled it perfectly and had used it to out-manoeuvre her again.

But perhaps she wasn't quite checkmated after all, she thought as the car came to a halt outside her flat. Instead he had given her a weapon that she could use every bit as cleverly as he had done. The soft purr of the Jaguar's engine had scarcely died away before she unfastened her seatbelt and turned to face him.

'I'm sure you won't mind if I don't invite you in.' Clea glanced ostentatiously at her watch and gave a falsely sweet smile. 'It wouldn't be worth it just for a quarter of an hour.'

Was that glint in his eyes amusement or anger? She couldn't judge, but she had little hope of his conceding her victory without further argument.

She was right, one dark eyebrow lifted, ironically questioning.

'Tell me,' drawled Matt sardonically, 'just what *does* happen to you at midnight? Do you turn back into a pumpkin?'

'I need my sleep.' Clea tried another smile, but there was no perceptible softening of Matt's hard face in response.

'So you've said.' His tone was a blend of one part dry amusement to two parts exasperation. 'But don't you ever ease up on this rigorous regime you've set yourself? Everyone has to enjoy themselves some time.'

'I enjoyed myself tonight!' Clea's voice lifted in indignation.

'Sure you did!' was the impatient response. 'When you

weren't counting the calories or checking that that bloody mask you wear hadn't slipped a tiny bit.'

'What mask?' Anger, uncertainty and the lingering discomfort of a guilty conscience where Liz was concerned all combined to put a tremor into Clea's voice that she heard with a sense of dismay. It gave far too much away, but she couldn't help it, her stomach was clenching nervously at the thought that perhaps Matt had seen through her, that he had known all along exactly who she was.

'That warpaint you're covered in. Damnation, woman, are you incapable of passing a mirror without looking at yourself in it?'

Clea's temper sparked at the biting contempt of Matt's tone, irritation mixing with relief at the realisation that her fears had been unfounded to produce a volatile mixture of emotions that could swing either way to fury or unhappiness at the slightest push so that she rushed into speech without thinking.

'I suppose you'd rather I was like Liz, dowdy and old-fashioned, not caring about my appearance at all.'

She regretted her words as soon as she'd uttered them, a wave of guilt at her unfairness to Liz sweeping through her, making her feel petty and frankly rather bitchy. What was it about Matt that always seemed to bring out the worst side of her character? She longed to retract the horrible things she'd said, but one glance at Matt had the words drying in her throat as she saw the black anger that distorted his face. The look he flung her would have frozen a volcano.

'At least Liz is genuine!' he snarled. 'She lets people see her as she is—she doesn't have to hide behind a coating of paint.'

'I'm not hiding!' Clea declared vehemently, rather too vehemently perhaps, but the way his words had come perilously close to the truth had destroyed her ability to control her voice.

'Aren't you? Then tell me, why were you so damn uneasy when I brought your watch back? You were like a cat on hot bricks, barely able to string two coherent words together—and all because you were afraid to be seen without your public face on!'

'Oh, now you're just being ridiculous!'

If only he knew the truth! Clea felt as if she was being dragged in two directions at once, not knowing whether to feel relieved that Matt didn't suspect that she had been so uneasy because she had convinced herself that he had gone out of her life for good, destroying her hopes of revenge, or to be angry that he should put her behaviour down to the vain, self-centred reasons he had given.

'I didn't expect you to come back, that's all. You took me by surprise.'

'And what sort of a surprise was it?' Matt stunned her by asking. 'Did you want me to come back?'

Oh, how did she answer that? To Clea's consternation no easy response came to mind. She knew what she should say, if she was going to stick to her plan then she should say yes, of course she'd wanted him to come back, that she'd have been disappointed if he hadn't, but if she told the truth——

A haze of confusion clouded her thoughts. What was the truth? Only a very short time ago she would have said that the last thing she wanted was Matt Highland's unsettling presence in her life, but now things were no longer so simple. She had come, if not exactly to enjoy Matt's company, then to find it stimulating and exciting. He emanated an energy that was impossible to ignore, and the days when he hadn't contacted her, when she had thought that she would never see him again had seemed strangely flat and dull, and she had experienced a totally unexpected thrill of anticipation as she had prepared for this evening—but that was because she was one step nearer achieving her aim, she told herself, nothing more.

'Well?' demanded Matt 'What's your answer, Clea? Do you want to continue with this relationship or do we call a halt right here and now and go our separate ways?'

'No.' The word slipped out without her quite being aware that she had formed it. She'd come this far, she rationalised, it would be pointless to turn back now, a waste of everything she'd achieved. 'I'd like to see you again, Matt, really I would.'

It was a struggle to meet those dark eyes with any degree of confidence. She was sure her muddled feelings must show in her face. Her mumbled statement was greeted with a small and, to her mind, infuriatingly triumphant smile. Clearly he had anticipated her agreement.

Damn the man! she thought furiously, strongly tempted to retract her words immediately. He was so self-satisfied, so arrogant! He had never seriously believed that she might not want to see him again. Well, she would disillusion him on that score—and the sooner the better as far as she was concerned.

'Then I'll give you a ring during the week and we'll arrange something.' Matt's tone was nonchalant, and a sharp sense of pique stabbed at Clea at the thought that her agreement meant so little to him. She was going to have to work much harder if she hoped to ensnare him deeply enough for her ultimate rejection to have the impact she wanted. With that thought uppermost in her mind, she turned to Matt once more.

'I didn't mean what I said about Liz—I'm sorry.' She didn't have to make any effort to inject sincerity into her voice, she was genuinely ashamed of her unkind words.

Matt accepted her apology with a slight inclination of his head.

'Of course you didn't,' he agreed drily, and Clea had to make a special effort to ignore the sardonic irony of his tone.

'Please tell her how much I enjoyed this evening.'

Carefully calculating the effect she wanted to create, she lifted her hand and laid it against his cheek as she looked deep into those dark grey eyes.

'I *did* enjoy it, Matt.' She made her voice as husky and enticing as she could, and was particularly pleased with the small gesture. It made it seem as though she couldn't resist the temptation to touch him. Matt's response was everything she could have hoped for. His eyes darkened until they were almost black, one hand moved swiftly to release his seatbelt, and he turned in his seat, his hands closing over her shoulders to draw her towards him.

His kiss was long and sweet and slow, and Clea had no difficulty in responding to it, her mouth softening under Matt's as her hand smoothed his cheek, a disturbing tingling sensation running up her fingers as she felt the warmth of his skin beneath her touch, the hard strength of his cheekbones and jaw. She let herself soften against him, coming close up against his firm chest, her nostrils filled with the scent of his body, its heat reaching her through the fine silk of her dress.

Matt's mouth left hers and slid upwards over her face, the lids of her closed eyes, and there was a strange pounding in her ears, a sound that she suddenly realised was the beat of her own heart, thudding heavily in response to the caress of his hands as they moved over her body sending her blood rushing through her veins. When his fingers closed over the soft curve of one breast she gave a small, gasping cry of shock at the fire that flooded through her, making her glow from head to toe as if she was bathed in the heat of a summer sun, not the cool light of the full moon that shone high in the sky.

'Clea,' Matt's voice whispered in her ear. 'Clea, my lovely, let's go inside so we can finish this in comfort.'

Immediately something close to panic gripped her. This was not how she had planned it at all! Things were moving much too fast for her, not least her own reactions, which had taken her completely by surprise, leaving her stunned and without the control that was vital if she was to carry out her plan successfully. She stiffened in Matt's arms, trying frantically to think of some way to end this situation before it got completely out of hand, fighting against the sensations in her body that told her that to end it was the last thing she wanted. Then, dimly, she heard a church clock in the distance striking the hour and, in a last-ditch effort to distance herself from Matt and the growing, burning need his hands were awakening in her, she began to count the strokes—one—two—three . . .

'Ten, eleven, twelve——'

To her complete consternation she realised that the words were not just in her mind, but Matt had counted them aloud, lifting his head to look down into her eyes, a darkly satirical smile on his face.

'Midnight,' he murmured with silky irony. 'And you're still out and nothing terrible has happened. You didn't turn back into a pumpkin—or was it a mouse? I can't remember.'

Privately Clea thought that the Cinderella joke had worn rather thin, but she choked back the irritable words that rose to her lips as she gathered together the scattered shreds of her composure sufficiently to manage a cool smile of response.

'Neither,' she said, and was pleased to find that her voice shook only very slightly. She was surprised she could speak at all, her mouth was so dry and her heart was still beating in double-quick time. There was an uncomfortable ache deep inside her as the excitement Matt's caresses had aroused ebbed away, leaving a nagging sense of loss that was totally bewildering.

How had he done this to her? Why should she react in this way with someone she didn't even like when other, much more pleasant men had had little or no effect on her? It was just technique, she told herself. Matt was an experienced and—yes, she made herself admit it—a skilful lover. He knew all the right buttons to press, the right moves to make, and like a foolish, naïve adolescent, she had responded instinctively. Somehow Matt had touched a vein of sensuality that she didn't even know she possessed, but simple physical desire was all it was—if there was anything simple about desire. It had nothing to do with feeling, nothing at all. Switching on a bright smile, she looked up into his shadowed face only inches above her own.

'It was the coach that became a pumpkin and the horses changed into mice.' Her confidence grew as the storm of emotion receded, her head clearing as the red haze that had filled it faded and her smile widened as she slanted a teasing glance at Matt's position behind the wheel of the car. 'And of course the coachman was a *rat.*' She emphasised the last word wickedly.

Matt's laughter was an unexpected and, Clea admitted, a surprisingly attractive sound in the silence of the night.

'So that's what you think of me—it's not very flattering!'

His grip loosened, releasing her, and Clea sank thankfully

back in her seat, her hands going automatically to smooth her hair where his caressing hands had ruffled it.

'Is that really how you see me?' Matt's voice seemed suddenly different, the husky note in it giving it a disturbingly appealing quality that she was determined to ignore.

Yes, you're a rat, Matt Highland, she told him in the privacy of her own thoughts, a sleek, dark, sophisticated rat perhaps, but a rat all the same—vicious and unpleasant and thoroughly untrustworthy.

'I don't know what I think of you.' Had she really said that? Clea could hardly believe she had spoken the words, they were so very different from what she had been thinking. 'Give me time to get to know you better and then I'll be able to tell you.'

'Time?' Matt echoed softly. 'All right, my lovely Clea, I'll give you time—— But don't take too long. I'm not a patient man. When I see something I want I go for it, and I don't let anything stand in my way.'

'When I see something I want I go for it, and I don't let anything stand in my way.' Matt's words echoed over and over in Clea's head long after she had gone to bed—but not to sleep, her thoughts kept her wide awake, staring blindly into the darkness. The implication behind that determined statement was obvious—Matt wanted *her*—and that knowledge should have brought a smile of satisfaction at the realisation that she was well on her way towards her goal of revenge. But at the same time, remembering the steely glint in Matt's eyes, the firmness of his voice, she couldn't help wondering if she had bitten off more than she could chew, and that uncertainty didn't make for peace of mind or relaxed rest when eventually she drifted off to sleep.

CHAPTER SEVEN

'COME IN, Liz, it's lovely to see you.' Clea held the door open wide, a welcoming smile on her face. 'I was just making coffee. Do you want a cup or are you still off it?'

Her smile changed to one of sympathy as Liz grimaced, wrinkling her nose in distaste.

'It still makes me feel sick,' she said resignedly. 'It's funny, isn't it—I used to down gallons of the stuff, but now——'

'Never mind,' Clea consoled her as she led the way upstairs to her flat.' It won't last for ever, and you must be nearly half-way through by now. How long do you have to go?'

'Four and a half months. Sometimes it seems like an eternity. I still get morning sickness and I feel so lethargic all the time. This hot weather isn't helping either—still, at least it should be cooler when I get really big.'

'It certainly will be in December.' Clea agreed laughingly. 'Would you prefer some fresh orange juice instead of coffee?'

'Lovely!' Liz sank into an armchair with a thankful sigh. 'Just what Junior and I need.' She touched her rounded stomach gently. 'At least I'm beginning to look pregnant. I felt a bit of a fraud at the start.'

'I know. I'd never have guessed if you hadn't told me,' Clea said over her shoulder on her way to the kitchen.

She'd never even suspected that Liz was going to have a baby, she thought, her mind going back to the first visit Matt's sister had made to her flat, recalling the long talk they had had, the instinctive liking she had felt for Liz turning into an open friendship with a speed and ease that had delighted her. At some point during that afternoon Liz had confided the news that, after months of trying and disappointment, she was at last pregnant.

Clea wrenched open the carton of orange juice with unnecessary force as she remembered her own reaction to Liz's news. She had been delighted for Liz because the other girl was so obviously overjoyed, but at the back of her mind lurked the memory of her first meeting with Chris and it had been all she could do to bite her tongue and not let her anger show.

'Matt tells me you're off to the cottage for a week,' said Liz as Clea placed the glass of orange juice on a coffee table and retreated to the settee with her own drink. 'I envy you. The Dales will be beautiful at this time of year.'

Clea managed an inarticulate murmur that might have been agreement. Unknowingly Liz had touched on a subject that had caused her much heart-searching and a good few disturbed nights.

When Matt had first raised the subject of a trip to Yorkshire, August had seemed a long way away. She had been sure that by the time her holiday came around their relationship would be over, just a memory with, she hoped only a glow of satisfaction at having achieved her revenge still lingering. But somehow the days had slipped by and Matt was still part of her life, though she didn't quite know how or why.

She had been out at least once or twice a week with Matt since the night they had had dinner with Liz and Chris. He had taken her to dinner, to several West End shows and even to the ballet, which Clea loved but in which none of her previous boyfriends had shown even the slightest interest, and each time he had been an attentive and courteous escort and had never left her without arranging another meeting. Clea had used every trick she knew, drawing on her extensive wardrobe to appear in her most stunning and flattering clothes, taking extra special care with her make-up and always using the excuse of having to be home by midnight in order to keep him dangling, tantalised by her elusiveness, but all to no avail. Their times together had been thoroughly enjoyable, they never seemed to run out of things to say to each other, and she was frankly amazed at the number of things they had in common, but, as far as her scheme of revenge was concerned somehow that vital spark had been missing.

For the truth was that Matt showed no sign of being so captivated that he put himself at Clea's mercy. There had been no repeat of the passion she had sensed in his kiss, and she had never felt that things were running away with her as she had on the night they had visited the Lawtons. If it hadn't been for the memory of that forceful declaration, 'When I see something I want, I go for it,' Clea would have felt like giving the whole thing up as a bad job, though it piqued her to suspect that Matt might accept her declaration that their relationship was at an end with a cool indifference that was a long way from the devastation she wanted him to feel.

And so when he had once more brought up the idea of a holiday in his cottage in the Yorkshire Dales she had seized on it as a last attempt to bring her scheme to fruition. This week would be make or break as far as she and Matt were concerned. If she couldn't entice him into some declaration of his need for her during the days they were alone together, she never could. She had wasted too much time on him already; she would do better to get on with her own life.

'Don't you think so, Clea? Clea?' Liz's voice broke in on her thoughts. 'You're in a dream! I don't think you've heard a word I've said!'

'I'm sorry. I was thinking——'

'Of my brother?' A mischievous smile curled the other girl's lips. 'I'm afraid he has that effect on a lot of women. I know he's my brother and I love him dearly, especially——' She broke off, obviously thinking better of what she had been about to say. 'But he's an incorrigible flirt and sometimes I despair of him ever settling down—though I must admit I've had high hopes ever since he met you. I've never seen him so taken with anyone.'

If he is then he's hiding it well, Clea told herself wryly, her mind a haze of conflicting emotions. She had felt none of the triumph she might have been expected to experience at the thought that Matt might be more involved with her than she believed, instead she was overwhelmed by a sense of desolation that had to be because of the loss of Liz's friendship that must come when she rejected Matt as she had every intention of doing.

'What did you say?' she asked to cover her disturbed feelings.

'I was just telling you how glad I am you persuaded me to have my hair cut.' Liz touched her soft brown hair, now shaped into a lighter, feathered style that flattered her small features much more than the heavy Alice in Wonderland mane Clea had first seen. 'Even my mother likes it.'

There was a note in Liz's voice that Clea had heard before when the other girl spoke of her mother, a stiff, unhappy note that was surprising from someone as open and caring as Liz. She had never seen the widowed Mrs Highland, but Liz had once shown her a photograph of her, a tall, superbly elegant woman who showed very little sign of her fifty-five years on her artistocratic and, Clea had thought, rather cold face. She had found it hard to see anything of Liz in Alicia Highland, but had thought she could see a great deal of Matt.

'Your hair suits you,' she said honestly, reflecting that, if nothing else, she had given Liz a whole new image in the time she had known her. Perhaps that would keep Chris's eyes from wandering in the future! 'And I'm glad to see that you're wearing some make-up, you look far too pale without it.' Clea considered Liz face critically. 'That blusher's a little heavy, though—and not quite in the right place.'

'I know. I tried to do it as you showed me, but I just can't seem to get it right.'

'I'll show you again, then.' Clea got to her feet. 'Come on—you sit in front of the mirror and watch what I do. You'll soon get the hang of it.'

They had spent a large part of Liz's visits like this. Matt's sister had been reluctant when Clea had first broached the idea of make-up lessons, but once persuaded she had soon entered into the spirit of things, trying each new technique with enthusiasm and putting the things Clea had taught her into practise when she went home. Like a keen student, she had asked non-stop questions, often ringing Clea for advice when she couldn't come in person.

'This is where it goes,' said Clea, touching Liz's cheekbones lightly. 'And the trick is to blend it over and over until it looks natural.'

At least she knew a great deal more about make-up than Stephanie had, Clea reflected as she worked, knowing a pang of embarrassment at the memory of the effect her schoolfriend had achieved on that fateful day nine years ago, privately admitting that she must have looked a sight.

Laughing and chattering like two teenagers, neither of

them heard the front door, which Clea had left unlocked, knowing that Maggie was due home any minute, open or the footsteps that mounted the stairs so that they jumped startled, when a dark figure appeared in the doorway and a cool masculine voice drawled, 'So this is where you disappear to, Liz! Chris has been going frantic imagining all sorts of dreadful things happening to you. I had a struggle to stop him ringing the hospital to find out if you'd had an accident. He said you were due to meet him over an hour ago.'

'An hour!' Liz was on her feet immediately, reaching up to pull the make-up cape from round her neck. 'I don't know where the time's gone. Sorry, Clea, but I have to go——'

'But I haven't finished yet!' protested Clea, privately taking the liberty of doubting that Chris was in anything like the state Matt had described. 'Can't you just——'

'No, she can't,' Matt cut in firmly, the cold edge to his voice drawing Clea's gaze to him so that for the first time she saw the dark anger that burned in his eyes, an anger that he was holding ruthlessly under control—for Liz's sake, she realised. A shiver of apprehension shook her at the thought that his fury was directed at her alone and she couldn't guess what she had done to deserve it. 'Do you need a lift home?' Matt added more gently, addressing his question to his sister.

'No, thanks—I've got my car outside.' Liz had already collected her handbag and was on her way to the door. 'Sorry to leave you like this, Clea, but you know how it is——Bye!'

As Clea listened to the hasty footsteps descending the stairs she couldn't help thinking that if Liz wasn't quite so devoted to Chris then he might not take her so much for granted. She would never let herself become so much at a man's beck and call, husband or not. That thought reminded her of Matt's presence and she rounded on him, her eyes flashing green fire.

'Did you have to spoil things like that? Liz was enjoying herself!'

'Perhaps.' Matt's tone was coldly contemptuous. 'But Chris was worried.'

'Worried!' Clea could not suppress a scornful laugh, but it died before an icy look from those dark eyes. 'Well, perhaps he was,' she admitted gruffly, unable to resist adding, 'but it'll do him good—stop him fancying other women.'

'Other women? *Chris?*' Sheer blank astonishment replaced the frightening cold anger in Matt's face. 'What the hell are you talking about? Chris is devoted to Liz—everyone knows that—but he's been very concerned at the way she's changed lately, and you're to blame for that, with your obsession with make-up and your appearance.'

'It's not an obsession!' Clea spluttered indignantly, her nerves raw from the scathing contempt in Matt's voice. 'I just like to look my best—and I was helping Liz to do the same. She wanted my help. She——' She broke off abruptly, remembering how reluctant Liz had been at first, the struggle she had had to persuade her.

'Did she?' demanded Matt seeing her hesitation and attacking straight at her weak point. 'Did she really ask you, or did you force it on her? My sister has no time for pretence or artifice. She's never indulged in all the tricks and play-acting other women go in for—until she met you.'

He was really angry now, his words lashing Clea like the sting of a whip so that she flinched inwardly. What had brought this on? What was so terrible about a few make-up lessons, a new hairstyle? Matt was behaving as if she had committed some appalling crime, but she didn't even know what she was being accused of.

'Now she spends all her time fussing about her hair, her make-up!' Matt spat the words out as if they disgusted him. 'She's changed completely, Chris doesn't know what to make of her.'

'Good!' Clea declared crisply, regaining some of her shattered composure. 'Now perhaps he won't take her so much for granted.'

Matt's reaction was a violent expletive, his exclaimation a blend of exasperation and confusion.

'Where the hell did you get that idea from? I know Chris, have done for years, he's never even *looked* at another woman!'

'Oh no?' Clea's voice was high and tight, the total conviction in Matt's words throwing her off balance. 'Then how do you explain that gesture! I'm not blind or stupid—everyone knows——'

'What gesture?' Matt cut in on her harsly. Then, as Clea hesitated, he exploded, 'Damnation, woman, you can't make accusations like that without evidence to back them up!' He took an angry step towards her and Clea fought against the impulse to shrink away in fear. Tall as she was, she found Matt's powerful strength awe-inspiring and, at this moment, frighteningly threatening. '*What* gesture?' he repeated forcefully.

'On the night of the fashion show——' Clea wished she had more control over her voice, it came and went unevenly, betraying the nervousness she was trying to hide. 'In the bar—he——'

Words failed her and she lifted her hands, curving them in the shape of the figure of eight as she had seen Chris do.

'*That's* what I mean!'

To her complete consternation Matt threw back his head and laughed out loud. His reaction was so completely the opposite of what she had expected that she could only stare in silent confusion until he sobered abruptly, that look of cold contempt wiping the grin from his face, leaving it hard and set as stone.

'Do you always judge so much by appearances?' he asked in a voice that was as harsh and unyielding as his expression. 'You damned fool—Chris wasn't fancying some other woman, that was *Liz* he was describing.'

Clea didn't dare voice her disbelief, but the look in her green eyes was frankly sceptical. Matt pushed an impatient hand through his dark hair.

'Chris was just telling me that Liz was pregnant.' Matt's voice was slow and clear as if he was explaining a difficult problem to a none-too-bright child. 'They'd suspected it, of course. Liz has always been boyishly thin ever since——'

He broke off abruptly, obviously changing his mind about what he had been going to say in a way that reminded Clea of the way Liz had done just the same earlier that afternoon.

'But once the baby was conceived she—filled out quite a bit. For the first time she had a really rounded figure and she was delighted about it. *That* was what Chris was describing.'

Clea knew her confusion must show on her face. She had no reason to doubt the veracity of Matt's words, his cold anger was proof enough of that, and she felt a fool for having jumped to such a hasty conclusion. But in a way Matt was partly to blame for that. Being the man he was, she had naturally concluded that his friends would be of the same type, a small, unrepentant voice whispered inside her head, but it offered no real comfort.

What sort of man *was* Matt Highland? She had thought she knew, but over the last few weeks she had come to doubt her own convictions. After that one forceful declaration he had made none of the moves to seduce her that she had expected and indeed had hoped for so that she could put her plan of revenge into operation. Instead he had been courtesy itself, his kisses light and gentle, his caresses only such as she could respond to with ease, never once had he pushed her further than she had wanted to go, which, after Simon's unwanted and demanding lovemaking, had been both a relief and a pleasure. But such actions didn't fit with that arrogant declaration that what he wanted he always got—so *did* he want her?

Carefully Clea slanted a glance at the hard, set face before her. Certainly there was no sign of love or even desire on that strong-boned face, and yet Liz had said—— Suddenly becoming aware of that fact that Matt was waiting for her to speak, she forced her lips to form the words she knew she must say.

'I—was badly mistaken. I'm sorry.' Her stumbling apology seemed to have no effect on Matt's anger, if anything, his face hardened further as he heard it, and Clea winced as a sensation like a burning flash of disappointment stabbed at her heart.

'I should damn well think you are. You've mentioned none of this to Liz?' His voice was harshly intent and his eyes probed hers as if he wanted to read the answer in her mind.

'Oh no!' Conviction rang in Clea's tone. 'I've said nothing!'

To her relief she saw Matt's tension lesson, the taut set of his shoulders easing slightly as he gave an abrupt nod of satisfaction.

'Thank God for that,' he muttered grimly. 'It would have hurt her terribly. If you so much as hint——'

'I wouldn't!' Clea cried urgently. 'Matt, you have to believe me!'

She was subjected to another of those searching glances, Matt's dark eyes burning with such intensity that she felt her skin might actually scorch where his gaze rested.

'Who was he, Clea?' he stunned her by demanding.

'Who was who?'

'The man—I take it it was a man—in your past, the one who messed up your life, convinced you that appearance was all that mattered?'

'I don't know what you're talking about!'

The sardonic lift of one dark eyebrow questioned her statement, setting alight a fire of anger in her mind so that she flung her next words at him in blind fury.

'And my past is none of your business! It's my own private affair, and I'll thank you to keep out of it!'

They weren't the words she wanted to say. *It was you! You're the man who hurt me!* The words burned on her tongue and she had to clamp her mouth shut hastily for fear she might let them escape.

'I'm making it my business,' Matt declared harshly, but Clea was having none of that.

'Then don't! You've no right, no right at all! You don't own me, Matt Highland. I——'

Her voice died, silenced by a warning flash from those dark eyes. She'd overdone it, she realised with a jolting sense of dismay. Provoked beyond bearing by his domineering attitude, she had let her real feelings show and by doing so had probably destroyed any hope of getting her revenge as she had planned. She might just as well have told him who she was and be done with it. One thing was sure, she could forget the idea of that week in the Dales. Clea caught her breath sharply as a twisting pang of regret told her how much she had been looking forward to going back to Yorkshire again.

'Very well,' Matt was saying. 'I can't make you tell me, but think about what I've said—you might learn something from it. And perhaps next week——'

'Next week?' The sudden lurching of Clea's heart made the words come out breathlessly. 'You mean—you still want me to go to the Dales with you?'

The glance he shot her from between narrowed eyelids was sharp, assessing, and filled with something she couldn't define, something that started a sensation like the flutter of butterfly wings deep in her stomach.

'Oh, yes,' he said in a soft voice that made her shiver just to hear it, 'I still want you to come with me. If anything, I want it more than ever.'

Clea was quite unprepared for the sudden rush of pleasure Matt's words brought her. It flooded through her veins like the warmth of the summer sun, making her skin glow so that unconsciously her lips parted in a wide, brilliant smile directed straight into those watchful grey eyes.

'Oh, good!' she said impulsively. 'I'm really looking forward to it!'

It was only much, much later that she admitted to herself that when she had spoken those words no thought of her personal revenge had entered her mind at all.

'What a lovely place!' The delighted exclamation escaped Clea's lips spontaneously as Matt's car rounded a bend in the winding, hilly road and she had her first glimpse of the cottage were she was to spend the next week.

It was much smaller than she had anticipated and sturdy, solid, rather than pretty, set against the hillside with lush green fields spreading out around it. Its dark grey stone came as something of a surprise to eyes so long accustomed to the brick and plate glass of city buildings, but it only took a moment to adjust, and as she did so a feeling of relaxation and peace filled her. It was like coming home.

The car crunched on the gravel of the small drive, then drew to a halt outside the white-painted front door. Immediately Clea got out and stretched luxuriously, drawing in deep breaths of the warm, clear air. It had been a long, hot drive from London and a strangely difficult one. She had tried to maintain some form of conversation as they sped along the motorway, but Matt had been taciturn and unresponsive, offering only monosyllabic answers to her questions and comments, so that in the end she had subsided into silence too and had contented herself with watching the built-up areas slip away as the countryside became more rugged and dearly familiar with each mile they travelled.

'You forget how fresh the air can be up here,' she said, and the lightness of her tone was natural, unforced. She could feel the peace of the countryside filling her, making her more light-hearted than she had been for weeks as she turned to smile at Matt. To her relief something of her mood seemed to have affected him too; the tautness of the muscles in his face had eased, and if she couldn't exactly call it a smile then at least there was a faint curve to the lips that had previously been drawn into a thin, hard line as he reached into his pocket for his keys.

Come and see inside,' he said, and the fact that the gruff, almost hostile note had left his voice lifted Clea's spirits even higher as she followed him into the cottage.

The interior of the little house was homely and comfortable, the two small downstairs rooms furnished with items that had a well-used look which made her feel instantly at home. In the living-room the deep gold settee and chairs looked soft and inviting, a stone fireplace housed an open grate and two walls were lined with bookshelves filled to overflowing.

'This was living-room and kitchen when I bought the place,' Matt told her. 'I had an extension built on to the house, a new kitchen and a bathroom upstairs. The builders used the same sort of stone so that it would blend in as much as possible.'

'It's charming!'

Clea was experiencing much the same sort of feelings as she had on her first visit to Matt's main home. After the sleek modernity of the Argyle, she had been pleased to find that his personal taste veered towards the traditional. She had never been able to relax in the glass and stainless steel sort of décor many of her model friends preferred.

'Can I see upstairs?'

The bedroom Matt led her to was decorated in cool green and white, the wardrobe, dressing-table and bed all made from stripped pine. The view from the window was the one she had just left reluctantly in order to come indoors, and with a soft cry of delight she crossed the room to perch on the wide windowsill and gaze out at the magnificence of the valley spread out before her.

'What a lovely place! I see now why you like coming here so much. It's so peaceful—such a contrast to London.'

Something about the silence in the room behind her stilled her flow of chatter and she turned uncertainly to find Matt watching her closely, an unreadable expression on his face. The ceiling of the small room was very low and his dark head almost touched it. He looked so big and strong that suddenly the bedroom seemed dwarfed by his size, and Clea felt a twisting of her nerves at the realisation that her response had been out of character for the woman she had appeared to be in London, the sophisticated career woman buried under the spontaneous outpouring of delight. Had she made a terrible mistake in coming here? Perhaps being in Yorkshire would revive memories of Patti Donovan in Matt's mind. Her stomach muscles clenched in anticipation of some comment that would reveal that his mind was working along those lines, but instead Matt moved silently towards the bed, dumping her case and the matching vanity case that contained her skin-care products and make-up which he had brought upstairs with him down on top of the crisp green and white duvet cover.

'I'll leave you to get unpacked,' he said, his deep voice not quite as firm as usual. He sounded abstracted, as if he had dragged his thoughts away from some very different subject.

'Thanks. I'd like to change and freshen up before dinner.'

Matt's expression darkened ominously at her words.

'It's only something simple my housekeeper prepared before I left London, not dinner at the Ritz—though from the amount of luggage you brought we might just as well be in some five-star hotel. For God's sake, Clea, don't you ever let up?—be yourself?'

'If being myself means wearing exactly what I like then that's exactly what I'm doing.'

Clea's voice was tart. If she admitted to the truth she had to acknowledge that the comfortable simplicity of the cottage had come as a distinct surprise. She had never quite believed in the country retreat Matt had described, thinking she would find something much more glamorous, something much more in keeping with the image of the sophisticated, high-flying businessman he presented in London, and the reality was having a disturbing effect on her. It reminded her too much of her home with her mother and Ned.

Her visits home had been rare times of relaxation, days when she could let go, dispense with the rigid regime she had to follow in London, and just be herself, casually dressed, her face free of make-up. An image of herself on her last visit, relaxed and carefree in old jeans and a man's loose shirt, the wind in her hair as she tramped across the moors, slid into her mind and she knew an intense longing to experience that freedom again but the knowledge that she could never risk doing any such thing while Matt was around set up a tension that made her muscles ache, and her mood was in no way improved by the sarcastic note in Matt's voice when he spoke again.

'I'll leave you, then. I thought we'd eat around eight—will two hours be long enough to enable you to look your best?'

Clea's hands curled into tight fists in reaction to the sting of his sneering tone, but she managed to meet his eyes with a cool smile.

'Two hours will be plenty.'

It was only for a week, she told herself when Matt had gone. Only seven days and then, one way or another, he would be out of her life for good. It was the strain of the pretence, she decided, turning her attention to unpacking her case and hanging her clothes in the wardrobe. She had found it far more wearing than she had anticipated and would be glad to be rid of it. She was going to find it even harder now, being in close contact with Matt every day, sleeping in this room, knowing that he was in the other bedroom, the tiny landing all that separated them.

Her hands stilled on the dress she had just unfolded. The separate bedrooms had come as something of a surprise too. She had anticipated that Matt would at least suggest they shared a room—and a bed. She would have swiftly disillusioned him on that point, of course, but at least it would have shown that he felt *something*—that he *wanted* her—so that she could have some hope of achieving her aim, without which this whole expedition was absolutely pointless. But what Matt felt, if he felt anything, was carefully hidden behind the charming, attentive, but ultimately passionless face he let her see.

With a sigh of frustration Clea pushed the dress on to a hanger and shoved it into the wardrobe with uncharacteristic carelessness. She had decided that this week was make or break, and her campaign would start right now. She would dress up to the nines, look her very best—and she knew just which dress she would wear. In a delicate peach silk, with a plunging neckline, it clung lovingly to the shape of her body, emphasising every curve. Determination drove her into action and she swiftly unpacked the rest of her clothes, refusing to let herself admit that, seen now, in these surroundings, almost every outfit appeared totally inappropriate to the sort of holiday Matt had planned. When a belated regret that she hadn't packed jeans and the sort of shoes she could have walked in in comfort surfaced she pushed it away ruthlessly. She hadn't come here to enjoy herself but to entice Matt into a trap, and for that she would need every weapon at her disposal.

Dinner was an uncomfortable meal. Matt had reverted to the taciturn mood of the journey and made no conversation at all but remained absorbed in his own thoughts, his silence setting Clea's nerves on edge so that she could barely swallow any of the meal he set before her, the savoury food tasting like cardboard in her mouth. But even her lack of appetite drew no reaction from Matt, and she was angrily aware of the way he pointedly ignored her appearance, making no comment on the dress and make-up with which she had taken such pains. For all the notice he took of her, she thought, irritation prickling in her veins, she might have been part of the furniture.

Things did not improve once the meal was over. As soon as the plates had been cleared away Matt picked up a newspaper and remained hidden behind it, not speaking a word, until, bored and furious at his behaviour, Clea announced that she was going to bed. Only then did he lift his head and give her a long, coolly considering look.

Instinctively she found herself stiffening, her muscles tightening in preparation for some sort of confrontation, and sure enough Matt glanced ostentatiously at the clock.

'You're early tonight, Cinderella,' he drawled mockingly. 'It's over an hour to midnight.'

'It was a long journey and I'm tired.'

Clea's voice was uneven, Matt's taunt reviving memories of other nights when, with some ironical reference to the Cinderella story, he had made certain that she was home before twelve. There had been times, more than she was willing to admit to, when his over-scrupulous attention to her impetuous words had irked her, cutting short evenings that she would willingly have let continue, and the memory of those nights stiffened her tone as she said sharply, 'I'll say goodnight, then.'

Matt acknowledged her words with a curt nod. 'Sleep well. Oh, by the way, I shall drive into town tomorrow to collect some supplies. I expect I shall be gone long before you wake up.'

The implication that she would lounge in bed while he was up and about sent sparks of anger flashing through Clea's mind. She should turn on her heel and walk out of the room she told herself, unable to understand why she was still lingering foolishly as if waiting for something. The realisation that she had expected—had wanted—a goodnight kiss shattered her tenuous grip on her self-control, and the way Matt's eyes drifted back to his newspaper was the last straw.

'If you're going to continue to behave as if I don't exist, I really can't see the point of my being here. I don't know why you brought me here in the first place.'

That brought those grey eyes back to her face, the coolly satirical gaze making her wish she had left things alone.

'Don't you?' Matt murmured silkily. 'Well, to tell you the truth, neither do I.'

CHAPTER EIGHT

'SO YOU'RE up, then,' said Matt, depositing a large box of groceries on the kitchen table, the fact that he made no attempt to hide his surprise doing nothing to improve Clea's mood.

She had woken ill at ease and unrefreshed from a restless night spent tossing and turning in a way that had nothing to do with sleeping in a strange bed or being unaccustomed to the still silence of the countryside after the noise and activity of London. Matt's behaviour the night before had angered and disturbed her, his total indifference, the absence of even a goodnight kiss leaving her with an aching sense of frustration that had kept her awake for hours. It wasn't just that his lack of interest threatened her plans of revenge, it went deeper than that, touched her innermost feelings, and left her feeling raw and bereft at the thought that, as a woman, she meant so very little to him. So it was as much to restore her own morale as with any idea of attracting him that she had taken special care with her appearance, dressing in a sleeveless pale yellow sundress that she knew suited her, its soft colour bringing out the blue-black gleam of her hair in contrast to its delicate shade.

But, once again, Matt had barely glanced at her, and now he continued without waiting for her to speak. 'It's a glorious day outside. I think I'll get started on the garden today—it'll need a fair bit of work since I haven't been up here for a while. Shall I take the lounger outside for you?'

With an effort Clea bit back the protest that rose to her lips, remembering just in time that it wouldn't fit in with the image she wanted Matt to have of her. As a teenager she had often helped Ned in the garden at home, and she had loved the long, companionable hours they had shared, had enjoyed the feeling of being close to nature and had learned a great deal in the process. She had been infinitely proud of the fruit and vegetables they had grown and would have liked to offer to help Matt, particularly this morning when she felt so much in need of some such peaceful activity to ease the tension that stretched every nerve. But Matt's tone had implied that he didn't want her help, and pride prevented her from showing how that smarted.

'No, thanks,' she said stiffly. 'I don't like sunbathing. I've seen too many tanned skins with the consistency of old leather to——'

She broke off, shocked and startled, as hard fingers grasped her chin and twisted her face round, turning it until it was directly in the path of the sunlight that streamed through the kitchen window. Matt's scrutiny was so intense it was almost like a physical blow, and she flinched in response to it in a way that had nothing to do with the bruising force of his grip on her chin. She had wanted him to notice her, but not in this way, she thought on a wave of near-panic as she saw the way Matt's mouth twisted savagely.

'Damn it, Clea, do you even know what you look like under all this?' There was a strange note in his voice, contempt mixing with barely controlled anger and something else, something Clea couldn't interpret, to roughen his deep tones and make them sound quite unlike his usual calmly confident way of speaking. 'You don't have to pretend up here—there's no one to see you.'

There's you, Clea wanted to say, but she choked the words back.

'I'm *not* pretending!' With a brusque movement she

twisted her head away from his confining grasp. 'And how many times do I have to tell you that I don't wear make-up for anyone's benefit but my own!'

The thought of the real pretence she was involved in, the one Matt didn't even suspect, made it suddenly very difficult to meet his eyes, and she glanced down at the floor, seeing one foot in its fragile leather sandal tapping impatiently, revealing her innermost feeling. It was impossible not to be aware of the contrast between her own slender feet in the impractical shoes and Matt's planted firmly on the tiled floor, comfortable in the battered trainers he had worn on the day of the picnic.

Slowly and irresistibly, as if drawn by some powerful magnetic force, her gaze moved upwards, over the length of Matt's legs in grey cord jeans, the soft material hugging his hips and emphasising the taut firmness of his stomach, across the strong lines of his chest and shoulders in the clinging white T-shirt and back once more to that disturbingly attractive face. The slight breeze outside had ruffled the sleek darkness of Matt's hair, making a lock of it fall forward over his forehead, and she knew a sudden almost irresistible urge to lift a hand and smooth it back, feeling the vital silkiness of it under her fingertips. Matt smelt of the sun and the fresh clear air outside that combined with the more potent scent of his body to have a devastating effect on Clea's heart, making it skip a beat and then jolt back into action at an alarmingly fast rate, seeming to beat high up in her throat so that she found it hard to breathe naturally. It seemed a particularly sharp irony that now, when she wanted him to be aware of her but had failed, she should be so intensely aware of *his* forceful attractiveness.

'Who are you, Clea?' Matt asked suddenly, the question and the soft intensity of his voice sending shockwaves of panic through her so that her eyes opened wide, looking huge and dark in her pale face like those of a trapped animal facing a hungry predator. 'Who are you really, under that careful mask you show the world? Where's the person behind the façade?'

'I really don't know what you're talking about!' Shock, confusion and sheer blind relief at the realisation that he still had no suspicion that she and Patti Donovan were one and the same person made Clea's voice quaver in a way that infuriated her, and with an angry shake of her head she pulled together the scattered shreds of her composure. 'Really, Matt, this is quite ridiculous! I would have thought that any man would be pleased if a woman made an effort to look attractive for him.'

'That rather contradicts what you said a moment ago.' was the silkily murmured response. 'I thought you—made an effort——' Matt gave the words a darkly satirical emphasis '—to please no one but yourself. And I'm not any man.'

And that was true, Clea reflected. In the few short weeks she had known him Matt had never been quite the person she had expected. Starting with his declared preference for the subtle blue dress when she had been convinced he would like the red silk one, he had constantly surprised and disconcerted her, and on more than one occasion she had found herself liking what she saw. In an effort to distract herself from such thoughts, and to divert Matt away from the disturbing topic of her appearance, she moved to the table and began to poke through the box of groceries.

'There's enough food here to feed an army. I'll put it away for you if you like.'

The narrow-eyed look he shot her told her only too clearly that he saw through her diversionary tactics, and for a worrying moment she thought he was not going to follow her lead. But after a few seconds' silence that stretched her nerves taut with apprehension he lifted his shoulder in an offhand shrug and nodded briefly.

'There are a few more bits and pieces in the car. I'll bring them in too.'

His voice was perfectly controlled, his tone smooth and even, nevertheless something in the way he spoke lifted the hairs on the back of Clea's neck in a moment of irrational fear. She had the unnerving feeling that in those moments of silence he had made some decision, one that affected her in some way, but she couldn't even begin to guess at what it was.

The box of groceries was half empty by the time Matt returned, Clea working swiftly and efficiently to put tins in the cupboard, perishables in the fridge. To her delight she had discovered a large assortment of different cheeses; clearly Matt shared her enjoyment of that particular food, especially Brie and Camembert which were her own favourites.

'That's the lot,' said Matt, dropping a bag filled to overflowing with fresh fruit and vegetables on to the floor and tossing his car keys on to the table. Then, with a swift, searching glance at Clea, he suddenly and quite unexpectedly reached out and picked them up again, sliding them carefully into the pocket of his trousers.

His action struck Clea as rather strange; it had seemed so considered and deliberate; and once again that frisson of apprehension shivered down her spine. But Matt's face was bland and unrevealing, offering no clue to his thoughts, his appearance apparently totally relaxed with no sign of the controlled aggression that had gripped him only moments before, so, dismissing her fears as fanciful, she pushed them out of her mind and continued with unpacking the shopping.

A couple of hours later she was curled up on the comfortable settee, deep in a book she had selected from the overflowing shelves. She rarely had time to relax so completely, losing herself in an imaginary world, when she was in London, and the novel she had chosen had absorbed her from the start so that she did not notice Matt come into the room and glanced up, startled, when he spoke.

'I've a question to ask you.'

'Yes?' Inserting a finger in the book to mark her place, Clea looked at him enquiringly, then her gaze focused sharply and she stared in confusion, unable to believe her eyes.

Matt had been out in the garden all morning. He had set himself the task of clearing a wildly overgrown section, cutting back the shrubs and depositing the branches on a bonfire he had lit by the back wall. She could smell the tang of woodsmoke on his clothes and his hands were grimy with dirt—but it was what those hands held that made her blink in disbelief. Dangling from those dirt-encrusted fingers was her elegant grey leather vanity case.

'Which of these things do you really need?' The question came curtly.

'What?' Clea stared in blank incomprehension. Matt's face was set in hard lines of determination and the dark eyes were like chips of flint as they fixed on her face, not a flicker of warmth in them. 'I—don't understand.'

'It's quite simple.' His tone worried her. It was cold and clipped, as unyielding as his face. 'I want to know which—if any—of this——' his mouth twisted and he injected a note of scathing contempt into his voice '—this *rubbish* is really essential.'

Clea's mind seemed to be working in slow motion. Matt's questions made no sense at all. On one level the answer to it was easy enough; one of the first questions they had been asked on the modelling course which had been part of her prize in the magazine competition had been which cosmetic they would most want to have with them if they were stranded on a desert island. But Clea could not relate that to her present situation in any way at all.

'What?' she repeated uncertainly, her stomach twisting painfully as she saw the grim lines around Matt's mouth tighten ominously.

'Come on, Clea, surely you can answer that! Look——' To Clea's shock and horror he turned the open case upside down and emptied it on to the rug before the fire, bottles, brushes, lipsticks and eyeshadow palettes tumbling in a disordered heap.

'What do you think you're doing!' she spluttered furiously. Most of her make-up was expensive; since she had made her mark in the modelling world she had bought nothing but the best. 'You might have broken something!' she exclaimed, dropping her book and getting to her feet in a rush to pick up the scattered items.

But she was pulled up sharp as Matt's hand shot out to fasten over her wrist with a grip of steel, holding her immobile for a second before he pushed her unceremoniously back into her seat, his eyes daring her to move again—a challenge Clea decided it was wiser not to risk taking him up on. Mutinously she sat still, only her burning eyes revealing her anger. Matt stirred the pile of boxes and cartons with the toe of one dirty training shoe.

'Which of these is *really* important, Clea?' he asked in a low, controlled voice that sent a shiver down her spine, his total calm somehow more frightening than if he had shouted at her.

'The moisturiser,' she managed, making a move to pick it up, then sinking back on to the settee at the sudden flash of warning in Matt's eyes. 'That one—over there.' She pointed with a finger that she shook noticeably.

Without a word he stooped and picked up the pale green tub she had indicated and tossed it carelessly towards her. She lifted her hands a little too late and fumbled the catch so that it dropped on her lap. With an effort she resisted the impulse to

snatch it up and hold it tightly in a defensive gesture as she
watched him warily, wondering what his next move would be.
For a long, silent moment he considered the multi-coloured
pile of packages on the dark brown rug, then, crouching down,
he sorted through them swiftly, his long fingers turning over
packets and boxes, his expression one of strong distaste as if he
was investigating the contents of a particularly unsavoury
dustbin. He selected a further two bottles—a cleanser and
toner, Clea noted automatically—and dropped them on to the
settee beside her, then scooped all the remaining items into his
arms and stood up.

'What are you doing with those? Matt!' she exploded as he
ignored her and headed towards the door. 'That's my
property! I want to know what you're going to do with them!
Matt!' she shouted impotently as the door swung to behind
him.

For a second she simply sat, stunned into immobility, then
as she heard the back door slam and saw Matt's tall figure pass
the window on his way into the garden she leapt to her feet and
hurried after him. She was running by the time she reached
the path that led from the kitchen door, her heart pounding
heavily. The sight that met her eyes as she rounded the corner
of the house had her slithering to a halt, to stand staring in
horrified disbelief.

The bonfire still blazed at the far end of the garden,
crackling merrily in a way that would have delighted Clea at
any other time. But there was no room in her mind for any
such feeling as she watched Matt throw first one and then
another piece of her precious make-up collection into the
glowing centre of the fire. Shock held her frozen as she
watched the flames lick round the casing of a set of
eyeshadows, its plastic covering bubbling and melting before,
with a sudden roar, the whole thing took light, sending multi-

coloured flames leaping up into the clear summer air.

'Matt—*no!*' Clea found she could move again, and she dashed forward as Matt repeated the process with another couple of items from the bundle as he held. '*No! Stop it!*'

Reaching his side, she caught hold of his arm, trying desperately to pull him back, but with an unflattering ease he shook himself free and tossed everything he held into the heart of the fire.

'Oh, no!'

Unthinkingly she moved forward, hands outstretched in the hope that she might be able to snatch something back before it was completely destroyed, but strong hands gripped her arms from behind, dragging her backwards.

'Let me go!' She struggled frantically against the steel-hard grasp.

'Clea, don't be a bloody fool!' Matt's voice was harsh. 'You'll hurt yourself!'

Heedless of his words, she aimed a violent kick at his legs, feeling a powerful sense of triumph as she heard his grunt of pain, but still his grip on her arms didn't loosen, and a moment later the bonfire turned into a raging inferno. Driven back by the heat, Clea could only stand and watch numbly as the hungry flames devoured every last item. She felt as if a part of her had, quite literally, gone up in smoke.

With a strength she didn't know she possessed she wrenched herself free from Matt's hands and swung round to face him, catching an expression of dark satisfaction on his strong-boned face. A wave of fury swamped her, her eyes burning vivid emerald-green, and without thinking she balled her hands into tight fists and launched herself at him, lashing out with all her strength. Her fists landed on his arms, his chest, but then as she raised her hands again Matt moved swiftly, catching her wrists and holding them tight as he neatly dodged another savage kick aimed at his ankles.

'Calm down, Clea,' he ordered coldly. 'You're hysterical.'

Clea flung up her head and turned a look of loathing on his calm face. 'I hate you!' she spat furiously. 'I hate you!'

Matt's dark eyes met her blazing green ones unhesitatingly, the coolly calculating look she saw in them acting like a rush of cold water on her temper, extinguishing the fire at once so that she stood immobile, trembling slightly, her hands still held prisoner in his. For several long, taut moments the only sound she could hear was her own ragged breathing, harsh and uneven in the stillness of the garden, then, lifting her chin determinedly, she spoke in a voice that matched Matt's in its icy tones.

'You can let me go now. I won't hurt you—I wouldn't want to touch you.'

The faint smile that crossed his face threatened her hard-won composure, but he released her without comment and stood back slightly, still watching her closely. As soon as she was free Clea turned on her heel and stalked away in the direction of the cottage. She knew he was following her, but she did not look back as she marched determinedly inside and upstairs to her room where she pulled her suitcase from her wardrobe and flung it on to the bed. Then, collecting a bundle of clothes from a drawer, she tossed them into the case with total disregard for their appearance later.

'What are you doing?' a sardonic voice drawled softly, and Clea flung a furious glance in the direction of the doorway where Matt lounged indolently, one hand behind his back.

'What does it look like?' she snapped. 'I'm packing—and I'm leaving as soon as I've finished.'

'And how do you propose to manage that?' The dry mockery in Matt's tone incensed her, all the more so because she hadn't considered just how she *would* manage.

'I'll take the car as far as the nearest village. You can——'
She broke off abruptly as Matt shook his head. The movement
of one hand into the pocket of his jeans reminded her of the
moment he had taken the keys from the kitchen table.

So he had planned all this quite deliberately! He had even
foreseen her reaction and taken steps to thwart her! Blazing
fury rendered Clea incapable of speech.

'The village is over seven miles away,' he reminded her
gently. 'And I can assure you that that case is hellishly heavy
when it's full. You'll never make it.'

Gritting her teeth, Clea ignored him, though her mind was
buzzing with frantic thoughts. Could she walk seven miles
carrying the heavy case? Furiously she cursed herself for
bringing only several pairs of high-heeled sandals with
her—they were not at all the sort of footwear for a long hike.
Perhaps if she left her case behind—if she made it as far as the
village then surely she could hire a taxi or at least catch a bus.
Even if she had to wait for hours——

'One other point.' The softly taunting voice broke in on her
thoughts. 'What will you do when you reach the village?'

'I'll cope! I've got plenty of money!' The lift of one dark
eyebrow, questioning her statement, alerted her to the fact that
Matt had something else up his sleeve, something she was sure
she wasn't going to like at all.

'You *had* plenty of money' Matt corrected, bringing the
hand that had been hidden behind his back forward so that she
could see what it held. A white-hot blaze of fury filled her
mind as she recognised her handbag containing her purse,
cheque book, and all her credit cards.

'Why, you——' She launched herself forward, trying to
snatch it away, but Matt simply held it tormentingly high, out
of reach, as he restrained her with his other hand;

'You bastard! Give that to me!'

He shook his head, the smile that curved his lips looking positively satanic in Clea's eyes.

'No chance,' he stated adamantly. 'This is going to be locked in the car boot—to which I have the keys—and I've no intention of letting you get your hands on it till I'm good and ready.' He gave Clea a none too gentle push which sent her stumbling backwards to collapse on to the bed. 'So you see, my dear Cinderella, you're not going anywhere.'

Through hot tears of frustration she watched him turn and stroll away towards the stairs. A few minutes later she heard his footsteps outside and the slam of the car boot, and knew that he had carried out his threat. Bitterly she accepted that she was trapped. Even if she made it to the village, without money or credit cards she had no hope of getting any further. She didn't know why Matt was so determined that she should stay or what he had in mind for her if she did; she only knew that, for now, he had won.

'I hate him!' she cried aloud, lifting her fist and slamming it down on the pillow. 'I *hate* him!'

But even in her own ears her voice had the false, unsteady ring of a lie.

CHAPTER NINE

'CLEA? Clea, are you awake?'

Clea groaned at the sound of Matt's voice, pulling the bedclothes round her defensively in spite of the fact that the bedroom door was firmly closed. 'Go away!'

'Oh, come on, Clea! You'll have to come out some time. You can't hide in there for ever. I've brought you some coffee,' Matt added, a cajoling note in his voice.

Even as Clea determined not to be swayed she knew she was tempted. She had barely eaten a thing since yesterday lunch-time, her disordered, angry feelings making it impossible to swallow more than a few mouthfuls of the meal Matt had placed in front of her in the evening. She had made herself go downstairs, refusing to let Matt think he had driven her to hiding in her room, and had maintained a front of icy politeness that had managed to see her through until the time when, with luck, she could escape to her bed.

'All right, sulk if you want to.' Impatience put a hard edge into Matt's voice. 'I'll leave the coffee by the door, but you'd better come and get it quickly or it'll go cold. I'll be in the garden if you want me.'

If I want you! Clea thought bitterly as his footsteps descended the stairs. Hell could freeze over before she would admit to any such thing! She would have liked to ignore the coffee too, but the thought of a warm drink was too tempting, and when she heard the back door open and close again she slipped quietly out of bed.

Cradling the mug in her hands, she crossed to the dressing-table and surveyed her reflection ruefully, scowling in distaste at the sight of her pale cheeks and heavy eyelids. She couldn't face Matt looking like this.

'Do you even know what you look like under all this?' His words sounded so clearly in her mind that she glanced up, startled, almost expecting to see his dark image reflected in the mirror.

She hadn't considered her face at all last night when she had removed her make-up, she had felt too raw with tension after all that had happened, thinking only of getting into bed and the oblivion of sleep. The action of cleaning her face was an automatic routine, one she had performed so often that she rarely even thought about what she was doing, but last night it seemed to have acquired a whole new significance. Painfully aware of the fact that the cleanser, toner and moisturiser were all that Matt had spared from the destructive conflagration and fearfully apprehensive about facing him again in the morning, she had felt as if she was stripping away the outer layers of sophistication she had acquired over the years and with them the Clea she had become, leaving the gauche and unattractive Patti clearly exposed.

'Come off it, Clea! You haven't looked like that for years.' Another voice, Maggie's this time, slid into Clea's thoughts, making her frown and look straight into the mirror again. Did she really look like Patti any more? She had come a long way from the garish, heavy-handed make-up Steph had used, it was true, and with her loss of weight had come a change in her features, making her cheekbones appear more clearly defined and giving her face an entirely different shape. But without blusher, eyeshadow, mascara it looked somehow vague, lacking in definition. Perhaps, in a way, Matt was right. It was some time since she had looked at her own face except in the way an artist might look at a blank canvas, planning the careful brush-strokes that would bring it alive.

Matt. The thought of him jolted her out of her reflections. She would have to face him some time, and she rather suspected that although he had left her in peace this time he would come back again—and she doubted that he would be so patient again. Perhaps the change in her appearance from nine years before would be enough to protect her from discovery—it would have to be, Matt had destroyed everything she could have used to emphasise that difference. She would have to take her chance, and if he did recognise her—well, quite frankly she no longer cared.

Matt was still in the garden when Clea finally ventured downstairs, but she had only just reached the kitchen when she heard the sound of his footsteps heading towards the house. Immediately she jerked into nervous action, fighting a craven impulse to run, and was at the sink, filling the kettle, as he came through the door. He stopped dead at the sight of her, his eyes going swiftly to her face and, with a tension that made a mockery of her earlier declaration that she didn't care if he recognised her tightening every muscle in her body, she turned her head and stared fixedly out of the window.

'Clea,' Matt's voice was unexpectedly soft. 'Clea, look at me.'

Mutinously she kept her head averted, but then a firm hand came under her chin and gently but irresistibly turned her face towards his. After one swift, flickering glance at him her eyes fluttered shut, her stomach twisting into nervous knots. She couldn't bring herself to meet his gaze, feared the recognition she might see in his eyes. But there was something more. That one swift glance had brought home to her the potent force of Matt's virile attractiveness in a way that threatened to devastate her already shaky composure. With the glow of the sun on his skin and the tang of the fresh, clean air still lingering about him, combining with the more personal scent of his body to assail her senses in a way that even the most expensive of aftershaves could never do, he looked stunningly, vitally alive and, painfully conscious of her own washed-out appearance, Clea felt naked and very vulnerable beside him.

'Oh, Clea!'

The gentleness of Matt's tone was a shock, making her eyes fly open again, and what she saw in his face made her catch her breath. His eyes had darkened until they were almost all black, only the tiniest ring of grey showing at the edge of the iris, and they drew her gaze and held it with a mesmeric force that blotted out everything else. The kitchen, the faint sounds of the birds in the garden, the warmth of the sun on her back, all faded into a whirling haze as she watched his dark head come closer, her lips parting in surprise and anticipation.

Matt's kiss was slow and sweet and infinitely tender, its very gentleness stunning her so that although she felt that she should fight, should twist away and tell him to take his hands off her, she wanted none of his caresses, she found herself incapable of movement. And in fact his hands *weren't* on her, she realised dimly. Both they and his body were kept well away from her and he held her still with only that gentle pressure on her mouth, and yet, delicate as that contact was, she could do nothing to break it.

He had kissed her before, many times, and yet this kiss was like none of those others, it was almost as if this was the first time Matt's lips had touched hers. It held none of the

burning passion of the night of the fashion show, and yet
there was something new in it that made her realise how
strangely unemotional those other kisses had been, almost
impersonal, as if Matt had been deliberately holding back,
keeping his distance during the weeks she had known him.
She had been able to convince herself that the yearning
response she had felt on that first night and again after the
dinner with Liz and Chris had been just a temporary
aberration, the effect of the wine she had drunk or an
uncharacteristic reaction to the stress of the pretence she
was involved in, but the warmth that flooded through her
now destroyed that comfortable illusion. She felt like a dry
forest parched by the heat of the summer sun, needing only
a tiny spark to set the whole thing ablaze, and when Matt
finally lifted his head she found she was trembling all over,
shaking like a leaf. The smile that crossed his face did
nothing to calm her unsteady pulse, and with a brusque,
jerky movement she brushed her hand over her face as if to
break the contact of his dark-eyed gaze.

'No, Clea.'

Gently he took her hand, pulling it away from her flushed
face, the light touch of his fingertips sending a sensation
like an electric shock searing through every nerve.

'I hadn't planned on that,' he told her quietly. 'But you
look so lovely——'

But that was more than Clea could cope with. Still
stunned by that kiss and her own reaction to it, she was
hyper-sensitive to the force of those keen grey eyes that
searched her face far too closely for comfort. Abruptly she
pulled her arm from his light grasp.

'I was just making coffee,' she said stiffly. 'Do you want
some?'

She was thankful for the few moments needed for the

small, practical tasks of collecting cups and spooning coffee granules into them. She needed time to pull herself together. Something had happened; something she didn't understand. She only knew that it had left her feeling as if her world had turned upside down and inside out and, try as she might, she couldn't revive the liberating feeling of angry hatred towards Matt she had felt the previous day, and without that she had no idea quite how to react.

In the end Matt made it easy for her. The coffee made, he simply launched into the sort of light, trivial conversation that she had no trouble coping with, some of her tension seeping away as she listened to his account of the progress he had made in the garden and even managed one or two comments of her own.

That conversation set the tone for the rest of the day. Matt was unfailingly courteous, offering only a pleasant, friendly companionship that Clea found easy to accept after the tensions of the previous day. He made no attempt to persuade her into doing anything, but left her alone, concentrating on his work in the garden, leaving her free to do whatever she wanted. Clea found this deeply restful. The slow, peaceful hours were in sharp contrast to the rush and bustle of her working life, the often frantic dashes from one appointment to another and then being passed from make-up artist to hair stylist to photographer when every move, every gesture, every facial expression was dictated by the demands of the camera. Gradually as the day wore on she became aware of what relaxation really felt like, and slowly she began to look at her career with new eyes, seeing how her success had taken her over, leaving little time for the smaller, more personal things of life and finally coming to realise that just lately she had often felt like nothing more than a puppet who could move only at the command of whoever held the strings.

Now she understood why Matt came to the cottage, why he felt the need to get away from London, from Highland Hotels and the demands his business made on his time. With that realisation came a sudden and inexplicable need to see Matt, and before she had time to consider what motivated her she was in the garden at the back of the house.

Matt was working on a heavily overgrown area between the two great apple trees, heavily laden with fruit, that grew against the wall at the far end of the garden. He had discarded his T-shirt in the heat of the sun, and Clea watched silently, her eyes drawn irresistibly by the play of muscles in his shoulders and arms as he drove the spade deep into the soil. His hair was tousled and the brown skin of his back gleamed with perspiration and he looked totally unlike the sleek, sophisticated businessman she had always thought of him as being.

'Be yourself,' he had said, and she had angrily declared that she was doing just that, but wasn't there another part of her, a part she had only just realised had been too ruthlessly submerged under Clea Mallory, successful model? With a growing sense of despondency Clea admitted that in other circumstances she would not be standing here, watching Matt, the few feet that separated them seeming like an unbridgeable gulf, but would be with him, helping him as she had once helped Ned. The ache inside her grew as she acknowledged how much she would have enjoyed that. But she had assumed a very different role and now she was stuck with it. To step outside that was to risk comparisons with Patti, to risk Matt realising how she had deceived him. The suspicion that perhaps this Matt might actually prefer, as a companion at least, the Patti she had left behind only added to her sense of unease.

Be yourself. With a frankly envious sigh Clea reflected that Matt never needed to consider being anything else. Even now, dressed only in a pair of well-worn, faded jeans and the scruffy training shoes, he had lost nothing of the aura of power and energy that always surrounded him. Those dark good looks of his, the finely honed body, meant that he had no need of expensive, stylish clothes or the other trappings that lesser mortals had to use to enhance their more ordinary appearance. Clea sighed again. Right now she felt she'd trade every item in her wardrobe for the chance to be properly at ease with Matt, to be able to share that other side of herself with him.

Slight as it was, Matt caught the sound of her sigh and turned swiftly. When he caught sight of Clea where she stood on the path he pushed one dirty hand through the sweat-damp hair on his forehead and, without speaking, smiled straight into her apprehensive green eyes.

Clea's breath caught in her throat. She felt as if her heart had suddenly stopped, then jerked back into action in double-quick time. It was crazy, it was irrational, but it was almost as if she had never seen Matt smile before, as if, like the kisses he had given her, he had always kept his distance before. But this smile held nothing back, it was warm and welcoming and lit his eyes as well as his face so that for a moment it seemed as if the sun blazing high in the sky had suddenly dimmed, growing cool and pale as an evening moon.

'I—I came to see if you wanted something to drink,' Clea stammered hastily, painfully embarrassed at being caught watching him like this and snatched at the first thing that came into her head to explain her presence. 'It's very hot. You must be thirsty.'

'I am.' To her relief Matt followed her lead easily, his voice smooth and pleasant, but there was something about his eyes that made her shift uneasily where she stood. 'There's some lager in the fridge that would be very welcome.'

It took only minutes to fetch the drink and after that she could easily have made her escape, but she found she was reluctant to leave and lingered as Matt gulped down the cool liquid, finally putting the glass aside with a sigh of appreciation. There was a streak of dirt on his lean cheek and Clea's hand had actually lifted to wipe it away before she realised what she was doing and, thoroughly disconcerted by the unexpected impulse, swiftly lowered it to her side again.

'What are you going to do here?' she asked with a nod towards the patch of the ground on which Matt had been working. 'It would be the perfect spot for a vegetable garden.'

'It would, but I'm afraid I can't plan anything so ambitious. I don't get up here often enough to keep up to something like that. I shall just have to turf it over.'

'That's a pity. Ned always——'

She broke off, appalled at what she had inadvertently revealed and, cravenly avoiding Matt's eyes and muttering, 'I'll take this in and wash it,' she grabbed the empty glass and fled towards the house. It was only when she reached the sanctuary of the kitchen that she realised that the look in Matt's eyes that had so worried her earlier was one she had seen before, on the night of the fashion show, just before he had taken her in his arms, when passionate desire had turned the grey of his eyes black as jet.

But why had it surfaced again so unexpectedly? Why *now*, when he had shown nothing of this during the weeks since they had had dinner with Liz and Chris? A cold shiver ran down her spine at the thought that she was trapped here with Matt, alone and defenceless. Her one fear had been that he would discover who she really was, but now she began to feel threatened in a totally different way.

'Was Ned the man who hurt you?'

The question came so unexpectedly, breaking into the light conversation Matt had kept up during the meal, that for a second Clea wasn't quite sure she had heard him aright. *Ned* hurt her? Ned would give her the world if she asked for it. Then the full import of the question struck home and she shook her head.

'No.' The rush of relief at the realisation that her thoughtless words hadn't completely betrayed her made her voice shake. 'No, that wasn't Ned.'

Too late she saw how her unguarded answer laid her wide open to his next question.

'Then who was he? What did he do to you, Clea?'

Caught in a trap of her own making, Clea could think of no way to answer him. If she had the courage she should take her opportunity and tell him the whole truth. Her foolish scheme of revenge lay in ruins round her feet, and surely if Matt knew who she was and why she was here he would be only too pleased to return her handbag and let her go. But her nerve failed her in the same second that inspiration came to her, and she seized on it thankfully.

'His name was Simon Blake.' She tried to put a wry note into her voice, but only succeeded in making it sound stilted and brittle. 'He was ten years older than me—sophisticated, experienced. I thought he really cared for me, but the truth was that he was attracted by the fact that I was the new name, the up-and-coming star in the modelling world. He wanted to be seen with me and he wanted a physical relationship, but I wasn't ready for one, so—he dropped me.' Painfully conscious of the hurt that had crept into her voice, she flashed a bright and, to judge by the expression on Matt's face, unconvincing smile. 'It's an old story. It's happened to hundreds of others before me and it'll happen to thousands of others in the future.'

'But perhaps those others will be able to cope with it better.'

Matt's tone had Clea stiffening in her seat. His words were softly spoken, almost sympathetic, but something roughened their edges so that her eyes went to his in surprise, seeing the yellow flare of anger in their grey depths.

Anger! Matt was *angry* at the way Simon had treated her! Clea's head reeled as she tried to adjust to this new and totally unexpected development, her abililty to think clearly shattered as, going back over what she had said, she realised that the stark little story she had told had been the simple truth. Simon had broken off their relationship because she wouldn't sleep with him, nothing more. The day she had fallen into the sea and destroyed the glamorous image she had believed he had of her, so long associated with his rejection in her mind, had had nothing at all to do with it. But what had Matt meant when he had said that perhaps others might be able to cope with it better?

'Clea——' He was leaning towards her, his eyes darkly intent.

'It was all a long time ago,' Clea broke in hastily, suddenly afraid of what he might be about to say. 'Long ago and best forgotten.'

But Matt's cruel words had been spoken even further back in her past, an unwelcome little voice whispered inside her head, long before she had even met Simon, and yet she had never forgotten them.

A light touch on her arm drew her startled gaze and she stared down at Matt's tanned fingers, dark against the whiteness of her own skin. He was too close, far too close, and those grey eyes were too seaching, too perceptive.

'Men like Blake aren't worth hurting for, Clea,' he said quietly, and the gentleness of his voice stung her in a way his anger or mocking satire had never been able to do. She couldn't handle his sympathy, not now.

As his fingers began to curve around her own she jerked her arms away as if she had been burned and, speaking simply from the need to fill the silence that had descended, said unevenly, 'I think I'd like some music—wouldn't you?'

Her heart sank as she saw the frown that darkened his face, but a moment later it was gone, carefully wiped away, and his voice was calm and quiet as if he was soothing a frightened bird he was trying to tame as he said, 'What would you like to hear?'

Clea found she couldn't remember the name of a single group or composer. 'Oh, anything—you choose.'

She regretted those words a short time later when, in the middle of the selection of folk songs he had chosen, she heard the notes of an all-too-familiar introduction. She had owned this record herself when she was seventeen, and in those first weeks after Barry had shown her Matt's photograph she had often locked herself in her bedroom, his picture in her hand, playing the traditional song, saying *Matt Highland* over and over again. The sudden rush of memory was too much for her and, heedless of Matt's surprise and concerned exclamation, incapable of offering any explanation for her actions, she got clumsily to her feet and fled upstairs. Matt simply let her go.

Long hours later Clea was still awake, staring sightlessly up at the ceiling of her darkened bedroom while in her mind the memory of that first meeting with Matt and the moment she had heard his callous words played over and over like some crazy film.

It *was* all a long time ago, so why couldn't she put it all behind her as she had surprised herself by being able to do with Simon? Telling Matt about Simon had brought no pain at all, so why did Matt's words still linger, festering inside her like some infected wound until they had driven her to this crazy idea of revenge? Why had a few critical words had the power to hurt her far more than Simon's selfish behaviour?

They hurt because I loved Matt—but even as she framed the thought Clea knew that was not the answer. The way she had felt about Matt Highland at seventeen had simply been a schoolgirl's crush, powerful and all-absorbing while it lasted but ultimately transient and insubstantial. So why——? And then in a moment of blinding clarity, as if a spotlight had been switched on in her mind, lighting up a previously dark and hidden corner, she suddenly knew the truth.

Matt's words had hurt so much because she had *expected* them. Because of her height and her size she had always felt something of the odd one out. The teasing of her school friends had reinforced that feeling and when, in her teens, she had become aware of the attractions of the opposite sex, her inabililty to wear the fashionable clothes she believed would make her more attractive and the thoughtless cruelty of the boys she had known had compounded the problem, building it into a huge inferiority complex that she had tried to hide behind the heavy-handed make-up and the wild, unflattering perm. Deep inside, she had never truly believed that Matt would see her as anything other than an overweight, unattractive teenager. She wouldn't have known how to cope if he had, she admitted ruefully. His words had devastated her not because she had felt that they were unjustified but because they had driven home to her something she already knew.

So what about her plans for revenge now, when the past had to be seen in this new and very different light? To her surprise Clea found that, having been restless for so long, she was now too drowsy to consider the question properly. Her last thought before she drifted asleep was to acknowledge with a touch of irony that perhaps she should have been grateful to Matt instead of hating him, because it was as a result of overhearing his damning comments that she had finally taken herself in hand and done something about her appearance. In fact she would probably never have had the successful career she had enjoyed if it hadn't been for Matt Highland.

CHAPTER TEN

THE SUN was streaming through the bedroom window with
the promise of another hot day when Clea woke from a
deep, dreamless and thoroughly refreshing sleep. As she
stretched lazily she knew an intense longing to be outside,
feel the sun's warmth on her skin, to enjoy this holiday
properly as she would have enjoyed the time spent at home.
She dressed swiftly, pulling on a pale blue T-shirt and brief
white shorts, and it was only as she made her way out into
the garden that she realised that she hadn't even thought
about her missing make-up but, in a reversion to the
freedom of her youth, had simply run a comb through her
hair and hurried downstairs.

Matt was at the top of a ladder, his head buried in the
branches of one of the apple trees from which he was
picking the fruit and tossing it down into a box that lay on
the ground. Silently Clea watched him for a while, then,
unable to stop herself, she took a step forward.

'You'll bruise those apples terribly if you do that.'

For a moment there was silence above her, Matt's face
hidden by the leaves so that she couldn't see his expression.

'Then why don't you help?' he said casually. 'If I throw
them to you, you put them in the box.'

'All right, we'll do it that way.'

For a time they worked in silence, Matt collecting the
fruit and passing it down to Clea, who placed it carefully in
the box. It was warm and peaceful in the garden and her
occupation reminded her of those times spent helping Ned

when was so much younger, so that soon she became completely absorbed, every trace of tension leaving her until she was completely and wonderfully relaxed. At last Matt called a halt and climbed down the ladder.

'That'll do for now. We've cleared all I can reach and I think it's time we ate. Thanks for your help.'

He turned a smiling face to Clea, but even as her own lips curved in an automatic response she saw the way his face changed as he took in her apearance fully, saw the swift darkening of his eyes, the slow, appreciative glance that swept over her, lingering with frankly sensual approval on the length of her slender legs in the brief shorts, and suddenly her relaxed mood vanished, swept away by the electric tension between them, its force so strong that she could almost feel the sparks in the air.

Only a few days before, she had convinced herself that she was fighting a losing battle by trying to entice Matt into being attracted to her. Every trick she had tried had failed, but now, when she had taken so little effort with her appearance, it seemed that he could hardly take his eyes off her. The irony of the situation brought a slightly wry twist to her lips because now, when she had what she wanted, she didn't know how to handle it. All she knew was that she had lost the bitter, angry feelings that had driven her to try to take her revenge and without them she felt strangely lost and vulnerable, a feeling that was made all the worse by the unexpected leap of her heart that told her how much she wanted Matt to want her as a woman, but in a very different way from the one that had motivated her for so long.

'You said something about food.' Her voice was as unsteady as her legs felt, the ground seeming suddenly not so firm beneath her feet. 'I'll go and get it ready, shall I?'

Matt nodded slowly, his eyes still on her face. Then, abruptly, he seemed to give himself a mental shake and the next moment he was smiling easily, the tautness disappearing from his muscles.

'Something quick and easy,' he said lightly. 'There's plenty of bread and cheese and fruit—we'll eat it out here. I'll clear up while you see to it.'

In the quiet kitchen Clea sliced a long French loaf with rapid, jerky movements, still feeing the effects of that electric moment of awareness. Nothing in her previous relationship with Matt had prepared her for the disturbing current that had flowed between them, making every nerve-end quiver in heightened response. It had to be the effect of the sun, she told herself. It had been very hot outside, and a glance at the clock told her she had been helping Matt for over two hours. It hadn't felt like that, she reflected. Somehow the time had simply flown.

Matt was lounging on the lawn when she took the laden tray out into the garden, and Clea found that the sight of his lean, relaxed body in a black T-shirt and jeans had an unnerving effect on her pulse rate, so that the tray shook in her hands, rattling the plates and glasses, the sound alerting Matt to her presence.

'Here, let me take that,' he said, uncoiling his long body and getting to his feet. His hand brushed hers as he took the tray from her and a tingling sensation like the feeling of blood returning to a numbed limb shot up her arm, sending a wash of colour into her cheeks so that she ducked her head, letting her hair fall forward over her face to hide her reaction from him.

They ate in silence, but a silence Clea found relaxed and companionable, until at last Matt stretched lazily and sighed his contentment.

'That was wonderful,' he said smilingly. 'You can keep your *haute cuisine*. For my money you can't beat simple food. It looks as if you enjoyed it too,' he added, his smile widening as Clea nodded enthusiastic agreement. 'That's the first decent meal I've seen you eat since I met you!'

A quiver of unease flashed through her. Lulled into forgetfulness by this new mood of peace between them, she hadn't even given a thought to the possibility that Matt might connect a healthy appetite with his memories of the young Patti, and she had simply enjoyed the fresh, crusty bread and creamy cheese.

'I—didn't realise how hungry I was,' she said stumblingly, then broke off abruptly as Matt, clearly misinterpreting her reaction, laid a gentle hand on hers.

'No, Clea,' he said softly. 'Let's have no talk of starving yourself at dinner to make up—promise?'

What had happened to the cold, hard Matt of two days ago? Clea wondered hazily. It was as if he had vanished, replaced by another man who looked exactly the same yet was so totally different that she couldn't believe he had any connection with the Matt Highland she had known. And how did she answer him? She felt torn between wanting Matt to know the truth so that they could begin again and the fear that if he did know the truth this new-found peace would be destroyed before it had really had time to form. Then she saw him smile and realised with a jolt of shock that, under the influence of his new, gentle mood, she had nodded agreement without being aware of what she was doing.

'Anyway, you'll work off what you've eaten,' he said getting to his feet. 'We've another tree to clear and it's your turn to go up the ladder. Coming?'

Clea hesitated, staring at the hand he held out to help her up. This was the man who had burned all her make-up in an act of such wanton destruction that she still couldn't quite accept that it had happened, she reminded herself. Only two days ago she had believed she hated him for that, for his arrogant carelessness of her feelings, his deliberate cruelty—— But then Matt grinned widely, his grey eyes sparkling with warm humour.

'OK, I'll go up the ladder,' he conceded, apparently misreading her hesitation, and once again his smile was Clea's undoing. She had to stay here, she was trapped she told herself in an attempt to explain her easy agreement, so she might as well make the best of things.

Clea's muscles ached, but it was a pleasant, fulfilled sort of ache, she reflected as she stepped out of a deep, warm bath and began to dry herself. It was a long time since she had worked quite so hard in a completely different way from long hours spent in front of a camera. In her bedroom she selected a simple cream dress, its square neckline supported by delicate lacy straps, and slipped it on, smoothing down the soft material before considering her reflection in the mirror. She could have looked worse, she decided. The sun had touched her cheeks with colour so that she didn't look quite so washed-out as before—but it was a pity she had no mascara to darken her lashes.

Biting her lip, she turned to look at the dressing-table, its polished wood top looking bare and deserted without the usual clutter of bottles and packages. The only thing on it other than the cleanser, toner and moisturiser Matt had spared from the conflagration was a spray of perfume. Reaching for it, Clea sprayed the delicate essence lavishly on the pulse points of her arms and neck, adding a touch to her ankles and behind her knees—because of the heat she had not bothered to put on any tights—before reaching for the sandals that lay beside the bed. As she bent to fasten the thin straps a sharp knock at the door startled her.

'Dinner's ready,' announced Matt, and at the sound of his voice uncertainty gripped her so that her hands were suddenly clumsy and she fumbled with the fastening on her shoe, unable to get the thin strap through the tiny buckle.

'Clea?' said Matt. 'Did you hear me?'

'Yes!' She was incapable of keeping the disturbed note out of her voice. 'I'm coming—oh, damn!' she exploded as her grip slipped once more. Behind her she heard the door open.

'Is something wrong?' he asked. 'You sounded distraught.'

Not half as distraught as she felt now, Clea told him silently. She didn't have to turn her head to see him, the prickling sensation as the tiny hairs on the back of her neck lifted in instinctive awareness told her only too clearly how sensitive she was to his presence in the room. Keeping her head bent, she stared fixedly at the floor.

'I can't fasten this,' she said unevenly, knowing there was even less chance of her succeeding now than before.

'Let me help.' Matt crossed the room and crouched down before her, taking her foot in one hand while the lean fingers of the other dealt swiftly and efficiently with the recalcitrant buckle. 'There, that wasn't so difficult. Now for the other one——'

He looked up as he spoke and as their eyes met it suddenly seemed to her that time had been suspended and this moment hung in a bubble of eternity, separated completely from past or future. Matt's hands were warm on her skin, his grip firm but gentle. He too had changed out of his working clothes, but the crisp white shirt and clean denim jeans brought no reminder of the sleek, urbane Matt Highland. The pale colour of his shirt added a new intensity to the shining darkness of his hair and with his skin warmed by the sun he looked glowingly, vitally alive.

'Clea——' he said softly, his voice suddenly husky.

With an effort that hurt her physically Clea dragged her eyes away from the hypnotic force of his and lifted her other foot so that he could fasten that sandal. She felt his fingers curl around her ankle, but he made no move to touch the strap on her shoe; instead he stroked the smooth skin of her leg, his caresses moving slowly upwards, and a moment later Clea caught her breath as she felt the warmth of his lips where his hands had been. She couldn't hold back a moan of delight as his kisses feathered across her skin; her senses swam at the delicate caress and she tried to fight the intoxicating feelings that were flooding through her.

Matt had trapped her here, she tried to remind herself, he had destroyed her property, taken her money, and was keeping her here, a virtual prisoner. But somehow she couldn't revive the anger she had felt, should still feel, and as if of their own volition her hands went out to tangle in the dark silk of his hair, his name a crooning sound in her throat.

In one swift, sinuous movement Matt rose from his position at her feet and slid on to the bed beside her, his mouth exploring hers with a demanding pressure that forced her lips open beneath his, allowing him to deepen and prolong the kiss in a way that sent a drugging delight spreading throught her veins, relaxing her taut muscles until she was limp and pliant against him. The narrow straps of her dress offered little resistance to his strong fingers as he slid them aside, baring the soft, creamy skin of her shoulders, his mouth following the path of his hands down to the scented valley between her breasts, the fiery trail of kisses unleashing a fierce urgency of need deep inside her so that she moaned his name aloud, her voice sounding thick and strange in her own ear.

'Clea,' Matt muttered hoarsely. 'Clea, I want you so much!'

'I want you too.' The words escaped her lips involuntarily. She no longer seemed to be in control of her body, her blood stormed through her veins and a raw sexual need that she couldn't suppress was directing her actions as her fingers moved to tug at the buttons on Matt's shirt, pulling them free from their fastenings, her hands moving on to his chest, greedy for the feel of his skin beneath her fingertips, the soft curve of her body against his inviting him to caress her as she was caressing him.

The few moments it took Matt to remove her clothes and then his own seemed like an eternity of waiting, but it was more than compensated for when she felt his flesh against her own, her body catching fire as he claimed her mouth once more. His caresses fed that fire, inflaming her need until it was a blazing conflagration of longing that made her feel she might almost die from her need of him. The feel of his lips on her breasts, his mouth tugging softly on her nipples, was an ecstasy so intense it was almost a savage pain, and she wrapped herself around him, mutely imploring him to release her from this torment of wanting. She had never known such passion could exist, never dreamed desire could be so all-consuming.

But a moment later she wasn't thinking at all, only feeling, feeling Matt and his warmth and strength inside her, all around her, everything other than their joined bodies ceasing to exist. Her cry of joy and Matt's hoarse exclamation of fulfilment rang in the quiet air as the crescendo of pleasure mounted to a blazing, shattering peak.

For a time they lay still, breathing raggedly, their bodies damp with perspiration, then Matt raised his head and stared deep into Clea's face, his eyes still hazy with the passion they had shared.

'God, but you're beautiful,' he muttered. 'So very beautiful.'

From some darkened corner of Clea's mind came the echo of those words as she had heard them in her adolescent dreams, and a terrible wave of doubt and insecurity swept over her so that she lifted her hands to her naked face, covering it from that keen, dark gaze.

'Clea, no!' Matt's voice was huskily intent. 'Don't hide from me!' Gently but firmly he prised her hands away from her face and held them so that she had no protection from his searching eyes. 'Don't you know that you're much more beautiful like this, without all that paint?'

Then as she made a move to shake her head in silent denial he held her still, one hand on either side of her face and repeated slowly and emphatically, 'You are *beautiful*, Clea. You don't need any artifice to enhance the way you look—you're quite lovely as you are—like this . . .' One long finger trailed down her unmade-up cheek and it seemed to her that never before had she felt the touch of any other man's caress with such a burning intensity. Her mind felt hazy and she found it hard to think straight. She couldn't doubt Matt's sincerity, it rang in his voice and burned in his eyes, but she knew her own face, knew that without make-up she was little more than ordinary.

'Beautiful?' she whispered unevenly, her voice barely audible, but Matt caught her question and smiled gently.

'Don't you believe me? Then let me show you.'

He levered himself up off the bed, taking her hand and drawing her with him across the room to stand before the dressing-table, pushing her gently in front of him so that he stood directly behind her, his hands on her shoulders.

'Look in the mirror, Clea,' he murmured, his breath warm against her cheek. 'Look at yourself—no,' he admonished softly as she tried to twist away, 'look at yourself, Clea.' One hand slid under her chin, lifting her face so that she had no alternative but to meet the eyes of her reflection in the mirror.

A faint gasp escaped her lips. It was as if she was looking at herself for the first time. Her black hair was gently ruffled around her face, giving her a softer, more feminine look, her mouth was a rosy pink after the pressure of Matt's kisses and her cheeks glowed with a soft colour that had no need of blusher. Above them, her eyes shone like emeralds, wide and clear, seeming larger than ever before.

Suddenly she realised finally and completely something that had been growing in her mind over the last two days, and a sensation like the fluttering of a thousand butterfly wings started up in the pit of her stomach as she recalled the times she had seen Matt's eyes on her, the fires of desire that had blazed in them, and acknowledged that it was only since the day of the bonfire, since she had appeared without the make-up she had believed so vital, that he had shown the ardent passion that had just swept her off her feet with the force of a whirlwind.

She had thought she had left Patti and her insecurity behind, but the truth was that her adolescent inferiority complex had lingered, shadowing her life—until now. Now it seemed as if the fire of Matt's passion had burned away that lingering doubt and at last she saw herself as he saw her. The woman before her had no need of any make-up, the face that had seemed so naked and plain without her skilled brushwork now appeared warmly natural and softly lovely.

Cinderella, Matt had called her, and in a way that was always how she had thought of herself, as the plain, dull creature transformed by beautiful clothes and the magic of cosmetics, destined, when the day ended, to become her former drab self once more. But Matt had given her a gift more wonderful than anything a fairy godmother could bring, he had driven away those lingering doubts and given her confidence in herself.

'Do you see what I mean?' His voice was low, huskily urgent.

Clea could only nod a silent response to his question. She saw what he had wanted to show her, but in the moment he spoke she saw something else, something that deprived her of the words to answer him.

Every woman in love is beautiful. From nowhere the phrase slid into her mind. She couldn't recall where she had heard it before, and any thought of trying to remember fled before a wave of shock that had her lips parting on a faint cry of bewilderment that she barely caught in time before she uttered it. Her own image blurred and all she could see was Matt's face behind her, his strong features, dark eyes and glossy hair coming into a new and sharper focus than ever before. Her mind too was crystal clear, as if a fog had suddenly lifted, leaving only one thought in her head.

She loved Matt, not as she had thought she loved him all those years before when she had been in the grip of an overwhelming adolescent crush, but with the truest, deepest, most abiding love of which the human heart was capable.

Dimly she recalled her original plan in coming to the cottage, the foolish idea she had had of enticing Matt into her trap, and then letting him down hard in revenge for the hurt she had suffered when she was seventeen. Now she saw things so very differently, and she knew she could never again think of carrying out that plan. Maggie's words came back to haunt her.

'Revenge has a nasty way of going sour. It can turn round and hurt you when you least expect it.' And her revenge had done just that, Clea admitted. Only a few short minutes ago Matt had wanted her every bit as much as she had dreamed of either nine years ago or when she had first thought of her scheme to get even with him. He had revealed his desire in every kiss, every touch of his hands—but he had never spoken one single word of love.

Clea felt as if a cold hand had squeezed her heart, twisting it in an agonising grip. Caught up in her thoughts of revenge, she had been blind to what was really happening to her, and now, too late, she knew the truth. She had laid a trap for Matt Highland, but in the end the only thing she had caught in it was herself.

CHAPTER ELEVEN

'LORD, am I glad to be home!' Clea sank into an armchair and kicked off her shoes, sighing her relief. Maggie smiled sympathetically.

'Tough day?'

'No worse than usual, but I don't seem to be able to cope with it so well lately. I don't know why, but I feel so tired all the time.'

Maggie frowned. 'That's not like you. I'd say you needed a break, but you've just come back from a restful holiday.'

Fiery colour washed Clea's cheeks at her friend's words. She needed no reminding about the week in Yorkshire, every single day of it was etched into her memory. In one way she supposed it could have been termed restful, certainly she and Matt had spent a great deal of time in bed—but what they had been doing could not be described as resting. The day they had first made love seemed to have sparked off an explosion of desire that could not be contained, both of them caught up in its force in a way that allowed no time for thought or doubt, no consideration of past or future, the present was all that mattered. There had been quiet times too, talk- and laughter-filled times, days spent exploring the countryside or simply working in the garden, but those hours had simply served to whet their appetites for the long nights spent in each other's arms. It had been a glorious experience for Clea, a few days suspended out of time when she could be with Matt, drinking in the sight, the sound and the feel of him in all the wonder of her new-found love.

But the idyll couldn't last for ever. They had had to come back to reality, and with their return to London that reality had hit home hard, forcing Clea to face it squarely. It was five weeks since their holiday, and in that time Matt had been a constant presence in her life. He was delightful company, a courteous, attentive escort, a passionate lover—but nothing more. Never once had he even come close to speaking any word of love.

At first Clea had told herself that she had no need of any such declaration. She loved Matt, couldn't live without him, and if his company and his passion were all that he could give her then that would be enough. But just lately the suspicion that it was *not* enough had begun to insinuate itself into her mind. Their uncommitted relationship meant that she was too vulnerable, too open to devastating pain if Matt ever tired of her. At times she felt it would be better to end things now, before she became deeply involved. Better to suffer the hurt now than to live with the knowledge that it must inevitably come some time in the future. But even as she framed the thought she knew she could never do it. She could never be more deeply involved. Her life centred on Matt, she felt as if she had only ever lived in order to love him, and without him she would be nothing. Even her work had ceased to satisfy her. She trudged through the days, coming alive only in the evenings when she was with him.

'I just can't drum up any enthusiasm any more,' she told Maggie. 'I never noticed before just how petty and self-centred the modelling world can be at times. Take something that happened today, for example—Althea lost her hairbrush—just an ordinary hairbrush, but she was hysterical about it. She accused everyone of stealing it deliberately. She wouldn't go through with the photo-session unless it was found.'

'Lord almighty!' Maggie rolled her eyes in amazement. 'A healthy concern for your appearance is one thing, but some people take it way too far!'

Clea's murmur of agreement was abstracted, her thoughts once again winging to Matt. *She* had taken things too far and Matt had taught her how obsessive she had become, bringing her up sharp with his destruction of the make-up she had once thought so important and which she now saw as nothing more than a frivolous extra. It was surprising how easily she had adjusted to wearing no make-up—so much so that the lengthy preparation for the photo-session today had bored her rigid and her face had felt heavy and stiff by the time the make-up artist had finished.

'And talking of looks,' Maggie went on, 'I know you say you're tired, but really you're looking wonderful these days—positively glowing. You have done ever since you got back from Yorkshire. And letting your hair wave like that was a stroke of genius. What does Raphael think of the new you?'

'He approves.' Clea smiled, thinking of the unrestrained delight the designer had shown when she had first appeared with her hair in the more natural style instead of the carefully cultivated sleek bob. In fact everyone she had met had remarked on the change in her looks—all of them approving, except—— Clea frowned, remembering something Raphael had said only that morning.

'I suppose this tiredness could just be the time of the month,' said Maggie, and her words combined with Clea's own thoughts to have her sitting upright in her seat, her mind working frantically.

'Have you been putting on weight, dearie?' Raphael had

asked, his boyish face marred by a faint frown of reproach, after a fitting for one of his sleek, body-hugging dresses. 'It seems to me you've got rather more up top than usual,' he went on, gesturing with his hands to indicate the curves of her breasts.

At the time Clea had taken little notice of his remark other than to resolve to check on the scales when she got home—something she had had little time or inclination to do since her return from Yorkshire. But now, considering the designer's comment in the light of Maggie's words, she came up with an answer that had her counting back dates in her head. That week in the cottage she had been totally unprepared for the storm of sensuality that had assailed her—unprepared physically as well as mentally—but, knowing how sick and miserable Liz had been in the first weeks of her pregnancy, she had never considered——

'Clea?' Maggie prompted, disturbed by her friend's silence. Then, seeing the look in Clea's eyes, she exclaimed, 'Oh, Clea, you're not——' She left the sentence unfinished, but there was no need to complete it. Very slowly Clea nodded.

'Yes, Maggs,' she said, 'I rather think I am.'

'You look, tired,' said Matt when she opened the door to him later that evening, and Clea struggled against a nervous desire to laugh because at this very moment tired was the last thing she felt. Since she had realised that she might be carrying Matt's child she had been keyed up, wanting to sing, to shout to the world that something very wonderful had happened. She had no doubt that she wanted this baby, wanted it more than she could say, and that thought had given her a new surge of energy so that she had been unable to sit still and had prowled restlessly around her flat, watching the clock, wishing away the time before Matt had said he would arrive.

But now, as she saw him so tall and self-assured in a black leather jacket, white shirt and black cord trousers, her euphoria evaporated like a mist before the sun to be replaced by nerve-racking doubts. How would he react to her news? He had never said anything about children, never expressed a desire to have a child of his own. Would he share her delight or would he—a shiver ran down her spine—would he be angry, hostile, thinking she had tried to trap him into a commitment he didn't want? All colour fled from her cheeks at the thought that he might use her pregnancy as an excuse to end their relationship.

'I think you'd better sit down.' Matt had noticed her pallor. 'What is it Clea? Aren't you well?'

'No—I——' Clea's tongue felt thick and clumsy in her mouth and no coherent thoughts would form in her mind, her composure vanishing as she met the narrow-eyed gaze he turned on her.

'Have you eaten today?' he demanded, his voice rough.

Eaten? Clea thought hazily, belatedly realising that, apart from a hastily snatched snack at midday, she had had no food at all. She hadn't even thought of eating as she waited for Matt, her nerves had been so tightly strung that she doubted that she would have been able to swallow a thing. Silently she shook her head, and heard Matt's exasperated exclamation.

'I thought you'd cured yourself of that foolishness,' he snapped as he shrugged off the supple leather jacket and tossed it over the back of the settee. 'I'll make you something right now—— No, stay where you are——' he added as Clea made a move to get out of her seat. 'I can manage. Would you like some coffee first?'

'That would be lovely.' Clea forced the words from a painfully dry throat. She didn't want Matt to make a meal, she knew she wouldn't be able to eat a thing until she knew what his reaction to her news was going to be. But Matt had already disappeared into the kitchen and reluctantly Clea subsided back into her seat. She couldn't talk to him while he was in this mood. Perhaps later, when he had calmed down, he would be more prepared to listen.

'Clea, where do you keep the coffee?' he called through the open door.

'The cupboard above the kettle,' Clea responded automatically. 'First shelf, left-hand side.'

A moment later realisation struck, hitting her with a force that had her out of her seat and into the kitchen in the space of a single second. But she had not been quite quick enough. The cupboard door stood wide open and Matt, a look of stunned confusion on his face, was staring straight at the enlarged photograph of Clea as she had been at seventeen.

Clea froze in the doorway, her heart thudding painfully. The silence before Matt spoke stretched her nerves to screaming point.

'*Who* is this?' he said at last, his voice hoarse and uneven.

'It's——' Clea's voice failed her. She swallowed hard and was about to try again when he forestalled her.

'Why do you have a photo of Patti Donovan?' he demanded, swinging round to face her, his dark eyes searching her face.

'Because it's—she's me,' she managed, unable to meet those probing eyes. She hadn't expected him to recognise the photograph quite so quickly.

'*You!*' Matt's eyes went back to the photograph and, following the direction of his gaze, Clea winced mentally, hot colour flooding into her face. Never before had the wild, frizzed hair, the garish make-up and ugly clothes struck her quite so forcefully. Seeing them through Matt's eyes she felt she could understand his reaction all those years ago. '*You* are Patti Donovan?' Matt's incredulity sounded in his voice. 'Barry's sister?'

'Stepsister, actually.' It was an effort to force the words past the knot in her throat. It was as if all the tangled emotions in her heart were forcing themselves upwards, choking her. 'Barry's father married my mother when I was ten and eventually Ned adopted me.' And suddenly the words were tumbling over each other in her haste to have the truth out in the open at last. 'Patti was just a nickname—Barry's name for me—but then everyone started to use it. At home I was always Patti, never Clea.' Her voice faltered, faded, as she saw the dark frown on Matt's face.

'Why the hell didn't you tell me before?'

Clea swallowed convulsively. How did she answer that? She felt as if she was trying to cross a minefield, never quite knowing when something might blow up in her face. A fearful glance at Matt's unyielding expression told her that only the truth would do, he would see straight through anything else.

'At the beginning it didn't seem to matter. It was all so long ago, and I didn't think I would ever see you again after that night at the Argyle. But then you made it clear that you were—interested—and——'

'And?' he prompted harshly when she hesitated.

'And then I didn't want you to know who I was. I wanted you to see me as a woman, as someone very different from that teenager you'd met all those years ago. I wanted you to want me—perhaps to care——' Clea knew she was becoming incoherent, but she couldn't pause to bring her thoughts into order because if she did she would never find the courage to go on. 'I wanted you to know what it felt like to be hurt as you hurt me then.'

'Hurt?' Matt's tone was uncertain, his eyes questioning.

'Yes, hurt!' It was impossible to keep an echo of the devastation she had felt then out of her voice. 'You said such terrible things about me to Barry—when he suggested I might work for you at your hotel. You said you wanted someone who would attract customers, not frighten them——'

A sudden change in Matt's face stopped her dead.

'You heard?' he said huskily.

'Yes, I heard! I was upstairs—the window was open—I heard everything!'

'Then——' Matt's shoulders slumped as if he was suddenly very tired and he pushed one hand roughly through his hair, his eyes never leaving her face. 'Then all this—our relationship—the time in the cottage—all you wanted was some sort of revenge?'

'Yes—no!' Clea didn't know how to answer him. 'Yes, I did want revenge at the——'

But he did not give her a chance to finish her sentence. In the moment she had uttered that betraying 'Yes' his face had closed against her, becoming hard as rock, and without another word he pushed past her into the living-room, pausing only to snatch up his jacket before heading for the door.

'Matt! Where are you going?'

'Out!'

'But, Matt—— Oh, please don't go. I have something to tell you——' But Clea was speaking to empty air. Before she could finish her sentence Matt was gone.

      *   *   *

'So it's definite?'

Clea nodded silently. She had heard the results of the test that morning. She was pregnant with Matt's baby.

'And what are you going to do about it?' Maggie met her eyes squarely. 'Are you going to keep it?'

'Of course!' Clea's tone was sharp. 'I could never have an abortion.' Instinctively her hand curved protectively over her still flat stomach.

'I just wondered—I haven't seen Matt around lately and——'

'No.' Clea's face clouded, her eyes becoming dull and shadowed. It was a week since Matt had walked out of her flat, a week in which she hadn't seen him or heard from him, and she could only assume that in his anger at the deception she had practised on him he had decided that their relationship was over for good. Well, she had expected it, but not quite this soon, not when she was so unprepared—but then nothing could have prepared her for the pain that was her constant companion every waking minute. 'It's all over between Matt and me,' she said forlornly.

'And does he know about the baby? Clea!' Maggie protested as Clea shook her head. 'You should tell him!'

'Maggie, it's my baby!'

'Yours and *Matt's*. You must tell him—he should at least be given the chance to offer to support you.'

'I can support myself.' Clea's chin lifted determinedly. 'I've saved for years. I have more than enough.'

'But Matt——'

'But Matt, nothing! Maggie, it's over—finished——' Clea choked on the last word as a wave of desolation swept over her at the thought of the bitter irony of her situation. She had planned to string Matt along then tell him that she was Patti Donovan, that she had only been using him out of revenge for his callousness, and in the end that was the way things had worked out. The one thing she hadn't planned on was falling in love with him—and that made all the difference between triumph and despair. 'Matt's gone out of my life, Maggie. I won't force him to come back just because——'

She was interrupted by the ringing of the doorbell, the sound echoing through the hall, going on and on as if whoever was at the door had put their finger on the button and kept it there. Maggie got to her feet.

'I'd better answer that—they sound determined to get an answer.'

As her friend left the room Clea hunted in her bag for a handkerchief and fiercely blew her nose, fighting back the hot tears that burned her eyes. Dimly she heard the murmur of conversation and then Maggie called to her, her voice sounding strange and uncertain.

'Clea, it's someone for you.'

Reluctantly Clea made her way into the hall—then stopped dead in shock at the sight of the tall, powerful figure at Maggie's side. She should have known! Some sixth sense should have alerted her! There was only one man who would have used the bell so arrogantly, like an imperious summons.

'Hello, Clea,' said Matt quietly.

'Matt.' Clea's acknowledgement was barely audible. In the moment she had seen him her heart had seemed to stop, but now it pounded wildly, the racing pulse of her blood roaring in her ears.

'I want to talk to you.' Those dark eyes were intent on her face, noting every flicker of emotion that crossed it, and with an effort Clea schooled her expression into one of careful indifference. 'Can you spare me five minutes?'

She could think of no way to answer him. A multitude of

conflicting feelings threatened to tear her heart and mind into tiny pieces, one half of her delighting in the fact of simply seeing him again, her eyes resting greedily on his lean, strong frame, the strong-boned handsomeness of his face, like someone who had been starving and was suddenly offered a banquet, while another, more rational part cried that she didn't want to be alone with him, that she couldn't risk it. She was far too sensitive to the sight, the sound, and even the scent of this man, and the recent confirmation of her pregnancy made her even more vulnerable. Instinctively Clea folded her arms around herself as if afraid that those keen grey eyes might detect some tiny sign of her condition. If she was to spend any time alone with Matt she might weaken, blurt it out without thinking.

'I don't think——' she began, but Maggie broke in on her hesitant words.

'If you'll excuse me, I left a pan on the stove,' she said untruthfully, and ignoring Clea's reproachful face she walked briskly into her flat, closing the door firmly behind her.

Damn you, Maggie! Silently Clea cursed her friend. I need you! But there was no calling Maggie back. Reluctantly Clea turned to Matt, becoming aware for the first time of the large, gift-wrapped parcel he held in his hands.

'What was it you wanted to say?' she asked, her lips feeling stiff and wooden so that the words came out in a high, tight voice.

'We can't talk here. Can't we go upstairs?'

Clea wanted to dig in her heels, declare that she didn't want to go anywhere with him, that he could say what he wanted right here—but Matt had already taken her arm and was leading her gently but firmly towards the stairs. Light as it was, the touch of his hand almost destroyed what was left of her self-control. The temptation to lean against him, let her hand rest on his as it had done so often in the past few weeks, was almost overwhelming, and a flash of panic at the realisation of how close she had come to doing just that made her snatch her arm roughly away. The trouble was that she did want to be with him—she would go to the ends of the earth with him if he would only say he loved her. But that was a vain hope, one that made tears cloud her eyes as she fumbled with her key, unable to insert it into the lock until cool, firm hands took it from her and Matt opened the door himself, standing back to allow her to precede him into the room.

The sight of her own familiar surroundings gave Clea a much needed boost of confidence and, taking a deep, steadying breath, she turned to him, glancing at her watch as she did so.

'Five minutes, you said. You've had two of them already—you have just three more before I ask you to go.'

'Sit down, Clea.' Matt was placing the parcel on the table and he glanced up in time to see her shake her head firmly.

'I prefer to stand.' At least this way she could look him straight in the face. His height and breadth were imposing enough at it was, sitting down she would feel far too overpowered.

'As you like.' He pushed one hand through his hair. To her amazement Clea noticed a stiffness about the way he held himself, a tautness of the muscles in his neck and shoulders that spoke of some inner tension. He seemed uncertain how to begin, she thought, then dismissed the idea as foolish. *Matt* uncertain—never! She wished he would hurry up and say what he had to say. His silence was stretching her nerves to breaking point.

'Matt, just why are you here?'

'I've come to apologise.'

Clea's nervous question and Matt's quiet words coincided exactly, so that for a moment she was unsure exactly what he had said.

'You've——?' she managed faintly.

'I've come to apologise.' His voice was stronger now, the words coming clear and firm, and a ray of hope pierced the darkness in her mind.

'For—what?'

'For the things I said to Barry about you.'

The small flame of hope flickered like a candle in the wind and died, leaving a black, desolate emptiness. He had come to apologise for the past, but to Clea the past no longer mattered. It was the future—her future and her child's—that concerned her.

'I didn't know you were listening,' Matt went on, his voice low, 'and—I'll be honest—I didn't realise how much my words would hurt you if you did hear them. I was thoughtless and cruel, and I'm very sorry.'

'It doesn't matter.' Clea exerted every ounce of self-control she possessed to ease the unevenness from her voice. 'It was all a long time ago—and, in a way, perhaps it was good for me to hear what you said. I learned something that day, learned how lazy I'd been about the way I looked—how careless. Really, I should be grateful to you. You made me take a long, hard look at myself, and I didn't like what I saw. You put me on the road to where I am today. I'd probably never have been a model if it wasn't for you.'

Matt shook his head slowly. Some of the tension had left his body, but his eyes were still dull and clouded.

'You'd have made it without that, Clea. You're beautiful—a stunning woman. Perhaps I gave you a push, but that's all.'

Ruthlessly she squashed down the soaring delight his compliment brought her. She knew he thought her beautiful, and now, because of him, she had never *felt* more beautiful. She also knew how much he wanted her physically, but that was not enough, especially not now when she was going to have his child. Pain wrenched at her heart and made her voice hard when she spoke again. 'Well, you've said what you wanted to——'

'No!' Matt cut in on her harshly. 'I haven't finished. There was something else I wanted to tell you—if you'll listen.' There was a new note in his voice now, a hesitant, almost diffident tone, and the dark eyes held a hint of appeal, one that Clea was unable to resist. She nodded her head in a stiff little gesture of acquiescence.

'I'm listening.'

Matt laced his hands together, clasping them tightly until his knuckles showed white, and a shiver of reaction shook her at the way this small sign of unease revealed the importance of what he was about to say.

'You've never met my mother,' he said, and his words were so unexpected that Clea could only shake her head silently, her green eyes wide and startled as she pictured the photograph Liz had shown her, remembering how she had thought Mrs Highland's face rather cold and proud.

'She was almost twenty years younger than my father and just twenty-one when I was born.'

Once more Matt raked a hand through his hair, a frown creasing his forehead, and a sudden pang of sympathy twisted Clea's heart. He was finding this very difficult, she realised and he was talking of something that meant a great deal to him.

'Mother was very much the social butterfly—she still is.' Sensitive now to every subtle nuance in his tone, Clea caught the fractional unevenness that spoke of the effort he was making to keep his voice neutral. 'I suppose, in her way, she loved my father, but she loved his money too. She adored going out—to dinners, to balls, the theatre—and she was very conscious of her appearance—her hair, her make-up—they're always perfect.'

He glanced at her and she caught the fleeting flash of raw emotion in his eyes. He covered it quickly, but she had seen it, and it made her hypersensitive to his tone as he went on.

'She didn't really want children, and particularly not a son. Perhaps if she'd had a daughter first she might have been different, certainly she found Liz a lot easier, but she didn't seem to know quite what to do with me once I was past the baby stage. I was too rough, too dirty, too noisy. The games I wanted to play would mess up her clothes, disturb her hair, so most of the time I spent with a nanny until I was old enough for boarding-school. Every evening I would see her for half an hour. By then she would have changed for dinner or whatever she was doing and I could sit and talk to her about my day before I went to bed.'

'Sit and talk?' Clea echoed faintly. 'But what about a hug or a cuddle—a kiss?'

The flash of savage anger in Matt's eyes was frightening and she was in no way deceived by his dismissive shrug or the offhand way he said, 'That would have ruffled her appearance. A kiss might have smudged her lipstick.'

'Oh, Matt!' Clea's heart ached in sympathy for that long-ago lonely boy who had been deprived of the physical closeness that was every child's right. She could understand now why he had been so hostile to her own obsession with her appearance, why he had burned all her make-up in that savage gesture of destruction. He equated such things with coldness, with lack of caring. 'And Liz?' Clea was unaware that she had spoken the words out until Matt answered them.

'Liz used to try terribly hard to be like Mother. She dieted until she was on the verge of anorexia, and Chris and I had a terrible struggle to make her eat normally. After that she reacted against everything Mother stood for, took no interest in make-up or anything.'

Until she had blundered in, changing all that, Clea thought regretfully. No wonder Matt had been so angry! He must have been terrified that his sister would revert to her old, obsessive ways.

'Because of this, I've always hated the way women place so much emphasis on their looks. When I saw you that day I came to Yorkshire I was revolted to think that someone so young and lovely——Oh, yes,' a small smile curved Matt's lips at Clea's start of surprise, 'even under all that warpaint I could see that one day you would be a real beauty, and I detested the way you'd spoiled that natural lovelinesss in an attempt to appear sophisticated. But I should never have said what I did, and when I saw that photograph and realised what I'd done—that I'd driven you to be so obsessed with the way you look—I felt guilty, ashamed, I couldn't face you, I needed time to think. I've spent all week thinking and——' Matt's hands lifted in a gesture of resignation '—I'm truly sorry.' His dark eyes, still shadowed by the memory of the lonely child he had been, met Clea's directely. 'Can you forgive me?'

'Of course.' There was no hesitation in her voice. 'But really there's nothing to forgive, I've already told you that. But I'm glad you explained. Now I understand why you behaved as you did—why you burned all my make-up.'

'That was something rather different,' he said, then, as if suddenly remembering something, he turned to the table and picked up the parcel he had placed there. 'This is for you,' he said, holding it out to her. 'To say that I'm sorry for that too.'

Clea's heart lurched at his words. Would she be a fool to allow herself some tiny, fragile hope?

'Matt,' she said hesitantly, ignoring the proffered parcel, 'what made that so different?'

But Matt shook his dark head firmly. 'Open the parcel first,' he said. 'Then I'll tell you if you still want me to.'

Clea's hands were shaking as she unwrapped the shiny gold paper. What she saw inside the parcel made her gasp in shock, one hand going to her face. One by one she lifted out the packages and bottles and placed them on the table. All her make-up, every single item remembered and replaced exactly. From a man who had very strong reasons to hate such feminine preoccupations, it was an act of the greatest generosity. For a long, silent moment she simply stood, unable to speak even though she knew Matt was watching her, waiting for her to say something.

'Clea——' he said at last, and the rough unevenness of his voice brought her eyes to his face, seeing his doubt and vulnerability written there clearly.

'Oh, Matt,' she murmured softly, 'I don't need these, not any more. You were right, you know, I was obsessed with my appearance—almost as much as your mother. What you did shocked me into realising that, just as the things you said to Barry drove me to think about my looks in the first place. Remember how you used to call me Cinderella? In a way that was true. I *was* like Cinderella suddenly throwing off her rags and realising that in her ballgown she was beautiful. But I couldn't see clearly, I thought it was just the clothes and the make-up, not *me*. You helped me see it all so differently. But I won't need all this,' she gestured to the pile of cosmetics on the table, 'because I'm giving up modelling. I——' She broke off abruptly, frightened by what she had almost revealed. Matt had explained his actions, had apologised for them openly and sincerely, but he still hadn't spoken one word of love, and because of that she couldn't tell him about the baby.

'Giving up modelling? But why?'

As Clea hunted for an answer to give him the memory of Matt's own words a few minutes before came rushing into her mind. Could he have meant what she prayed he had? She had to take a chance to find out.

'Will you answer me one question first?' she asked tremulously, meeting his frowning dark gaze with eyes that were wide with apprehension. At his nod she continued slightly more confidently. 'You said that when you burned all my make-up it was something rather different——' The importance of what she was about to say suddenly overwhelmed her and she couldn't go on.

'It was,' Matt confirmed and the sudden huskiness of his voice, a new softness in his eyes gave her the confidence she needed. Drawing a deep breath, she brought the words out in a rush.

'Why was it so different?'

The smile that lit his face with an unexpected warmth was reflected glowingly in his eyes.

'When I said those things about you to Barry I was simply reacting to what I saw as the spoiling of a potentially very lovely young girl—one I hardly knew. But when I burned your make-up it went deeper than that. I was destroying something that, once again, was keeping me from getting close to a woman I loved.'

Only now did Clea realise that she had been holding her breath as she spoke, and she let it go in a long sigh, her lips curving into a wide smile of deep contentment, her eyes glowing emerald-green with happiness.

'Do you love me, Matt?' she asked softly, and saw his eyes darken in a way that sent her heart soaring.

'Hell and damnation, woman—I'm crazy about you! I couldn't stay away from you from the start, even though, on the surface at least, it seemed you were the sort of woman I detested. But then that day we had the picnic, when I brought your watch back, I saw you as I knew you could be—without a scrap of make-up, so fresh and naturally lovely that you took my breath away. I lost my heart right there and then, but——' Matt's lopsided smile made him look very boyish and so vulnerable that Clea longed to fling her arms around his neck and kiss away his uncertainty '—I was afraid to tell you.'

And that she could understand. After years of having his childish gestures of love rejected by his mother, he would naturally be loath to lay himself open to such hurt again.

'Clea——' Matt's voice was husky. 'I have to know how you feel about me.'

Her smile widened. 'Oh, Matt,' she teased gently, 'how did Cinderella feel about Prince Charming?'

'Some Prince Charming!' Matt declared self-derisively. 'I bullied you, virtually kept you prisoner, burned your——' He broke off as she moved suddenly, laying a hand on his mouth to silence him.

'I told you I don't need that make-up any more. You didn't need to give it to me.'

'No?' His grey eyes searched her face and she met his gaze confidently, her own bright and clear with conviction. 'Well, if you don't want that from me perhaps you'll take this instead.'

He was reaching into his pocket as he spoke, pulling out a small jeweller's box. Seeing it, Clea found she was trembling all over. She could have no doubt what it contained and she knew that the time had come to tell him the whole truth.

'I had this with me the last time I was here,' Matt was saying. 'I planned to ask you to marry me then, but when I saw that photograph and thought that I was the one who'd driven you to become the sort of woman my mother is I felt guilty as hell—especially when you said all you wanted was revenge.'

His voice roughened on the last words and the look he turned on her was once more touched with uncertainty, an uncertainty she knew she had to erase.

'It started out like that,' she told him in a low voice. 'I thought I hated you, but then, in your cottage, everything changed. When you made love to me I realised what I really felt. It wasn't hate—it was love. I love you, Matt.' Her voice changed, grew stronger with the deep conviction she felt. 'I love you with all my heart. This last week I've only been half a person without you. I love you, I desire you, and I need you—especially now.'

A puzzled frown crossed Matt's face. 'Now?' he echoed questioningly.

Clea nodded, her eyes warmed by an inner glow. 'I need you to be a father to our baby.'

Her words were greeted by a total silence. As he stared at her, his face a picture of stunned amazement, a frisson of doubt shivered down her spine.

'You're—going to have a baby?' he said slowly.

'Yes—next May. Oh, Matt, do you mind?'

'Mind!' he exclaimed. 'I'm ecstatic! God, Clea, if you only knew how I envied Liz and Chris—— Oh, Clea, my darling, are you sure?'

'Completely sure—it was confirmed this morning. I——' The rest of her words were driven from her mind as she was gathered into a fierce embrace that drove all the breath from her body. Matt's hands came up to brush her hair back from her face with infinite tenderness.

'You've made me the happiest man in the world,' he sighed. 'You don't know how much this means to me.'

But Clea thought she could guess. With the memory of his own love-starved childhood behind him, he would give their child all the devotion and love it would ever need. Limp with happiness, she relaxed into his arms, letting herself rest against his strength, then as a sudden thought occurred to her she twisted round so that she could look up into his eyes.

'That make-up,' she murmured, not knowing quite how to form the question.

'Use it,' Matt told her, his eyes dark and sincere. 'Use it or not as you like—it doesn't matter. To me you'll always be the most beautiful woman in the world—the only woman—my wife.'

'Your wife,' Clea echoed in delight. The words had the most wonderful sound. Suddenly Matt's expression changed, wicked laughter dancing in his eyes.

'There's just one thing I need to know, Cinderella,' he said, coming so close that his lips were against her cheek. 'Do you really change back into what you used to be at midnight? I'd hate to wake up and find a pumpkin on the pillow.'

An answering laughter bubbled up inside her. 'You should know the answer to that! What about those nights in the cottage? Don't you remember?'

'I'm not sure.' Matt's lips were sliding closer to her mouth, his hands moving over her body, setting it alight with his caressess. 'Perhaps you'd like to remind me?'

'Willingly——'

The rest of Clea's words were smothered under the pressure of his lips, her last rational thought being a memory of the conclusion of the old tale in her childhood storybook— 'So Cinderella married her prince'—and she knew that, as all true fairy stories should end, they too would live happily ever after.

Harlequin American Romance

Harlequin Temptation dares to be different!

Once in a while, we Temptation editors spot a romance that's truly innovative. To make sure *you* don't miss any one of these outstanding selections, we'll mark them for you.

EDITOR'S CHOICE

When the "Editors' Choice" fold-back appears on a Temptation cover, you'll know we've found that extra-special page-turner!

THE

EDITORS

Keepsake

✦ Harlequin Superromance

Harlequin Intrigue

Two exciting new stories each month.

Each title mixes a contemporary, sophisticated romance with the surprising twists and turns of a puzzler... romance with "something more."

Because romance can be quite an adventure.

Romance, Suspense and Adventure